Phil 4:13

THE
LONGEST
NEW YORK
MINUTE

THE
LONGEST
NEW YORK
MINUTE

TRACY POPOLIZIO

TATE PUBLISHING
AND ENTERPRISES, LLC

Published by Tate Publishing & Enterprises, LLC
127 E. Trade Center Terrace | Mustang, Oklahoma 73064 USA
1.888.361.9473 | www.tatepublishing.com

Tate Publishing is committed to excellence in the publishing industry. The company reflects the philosophy established by the founders, based on Psalm 68:11,
"The Lord gave the word and great was the company of those who published it."

Book design copyright © 2015 by Tate Publishing, LLC. All rights reserved.
Cover design by Joseph Emnace
Interior design by Manolito Bastasa

Published in the United States of America

ISBN: 978-1-63063-764-4
Juvenile Fiction / General
14.12.15

ACKNOWLEDGMENTS

First I'd like to say an extra special thanks to my wonderful family. Nick, my beloved husband, whose unconditional love, patience, and encouragement during the writing process helped me tremendously, not to mention the best book title ever. I love you, honey. Thank you, Lexie, my inquisitive daughter, whose interest in this topic three years ago sparked the idea for this book in the first place. And last but not least, my little man, Daniel, who came to show a great interest in this topic as he sketched possible cover pictures for me. Thank you all for your support and believing in me.

Special thanks also goes out to all the people who spent their precious time pouring over this book, helping to make this book a reality. Specifically, thank you, Mom, for not just one but multiple readings, and all the time you spent sitting with me making corrections. Thank you, Sam, for your support, and to you and Mom for the unforgettable photo shoots—truly unforgettable. Dad, thank you for your unending support and encouragement through this process.

I also want to thank Mrs. B, whose teachings twenty-five years ago were brought back to the forefront of my mind. Thank you for your endless support and time pouring over the book. Thanks to Jess, who spent hours reading through it and sitting with me to push me even further. Thanks also to Michelle, Jill, and Abby for all your suggestions and support. Thank you to all the people at Tate Publishing, who believed in the dream and made it a reality.

I also want to especially thank Jennifer Fimiani, my cousin, whose firsthand experiences with the Red Cross trauma team gave me immeasurable insight into the tragic events of that day. Thank you so much, Jennifer.

Finally, and most importantly, I thank the Most High God, my Lord and Savior, who inspired me with the ideas and showed me how to transform them into words from my spirit onto paper. This entire piece of work would not exist without Him.

But those who wait on the Lord shall renew their strength; they shall mount up with wings like eagles, they shall run and not be weary, they shall walk and not faint.

—Isaiah 40:31 (NKJV)

CHAPTER 1

Exhausted, Jessica Bianchi grabbed the railing as she leaned over it to observe the grim picture below her. She closed her eyes and made a mental image, reminding herself to sketch this at a later date—a much later date—when the horror of the past twenty-four hours did not present itself every time she closed her eyes.

Opening her eyes to the banging of a door, Jessica craned her neck so she could see the doorway. Maybe this time would be different. Maybe this time that open door would bring the one thing that caused her to be at St. Paul's Chapel in the first place.

Unfortunately, it was more of the same. Dust-covered beings who moved automatically, almost robotically, their faces grim looking, only speaking out of necessity. Physically present, emotionally someplace else. They came in to the chapel to rest on one of the pews, or to force down a bite to eat, before braving their work once more. Nobody talked much, and when they did, it was in whispers. She didn't know if it was out of respect, exhaustion, or sorrow.

Since they all looked the same, Jessica found it difficult to identify the one particular person she was looking for. But she knew that when the time came, and she was sure it would, she would know.

~

Buddy Powers was never one to shy away from offering his help, no matter the circumstance. Today was no different. He had heard the news. Everyone had heard it. The Twin Towers were no more. Buddy, a steel worker in Upstate New York, was gathered around a small TV in his boss's trailer with the rest of his crew to watch the nightmare unfold.

"How'd they get in anyways is what I want to know," Bob Hill, Buddy's boss, asked anybody who would listen. "They're desperate to get help down there. Who's ready?"

~

Gripping the railing tighter, Jessica struggled with feelings of guilt and fear. *How did this happen?* she thought to herself. It wasn't that long ago when Jessica celebrated her thirteenth birthday in a place that now no longer existed. The sadness overtook her once more, and she allowed her thoughts to travel back to earlier that same year. Back when she thought she knew better than her parents, especially her father.

CHAPTER 2

The warm April sunlight streamed through the large glass, and Jessica had to squint to look up at all the flags that hung inside Tower 2, or the South Tower, as it was also called. She loved coming to the World Trade Center. Usually, Mrs. Bianchi would take Jessica and her ten-year-old sister, Ashley, shopping at the mall before meeting their father for lunch at one of the stands. Jessica especially loved it when they had enough time to go up to the observation deck and look out over Manhattan, the only home she had known for the thirteen years of her life. Thirteen years exactly. Soon her father would join them and they would travel up together to the 106th floor of Tower 1 to have a special birthday lunch at the Windows on the World restaurant.

Anthony Bianchi, a prominent banker in New York City, worked in the Deutsche Bank Building. Jessica wasn't quite sure what he did, but she knew that when she was ten, Deutsche Bank acquired the building from another company her father worked for first, and by God's grace, her father had been one of the fortunate bankers not to lose his job.

She wouldn't lie. After hours of tossing and turning, waiting for him to come home, Jessica wished he had lost it. Maybe this was selfish. Maybe she should have been glad he was one of the lucky ones: lucky to miss dinner with his family every other night; lucky to miss celebrations and school events; lucky to miss out on his daughters' lives.

Feelings of resentment had begun to pile up like a wall of bricks around her over the past couple years, causing a rift in the once tight relationship between father and daughter. Jessica used to lie in bed and wait for her father to come home and tell her all about the delicious dinners he had with clients while looking out over the city. He always told her that he could see their apartment building from his table and that he would blow her a kiss good-night. He made a date with the girls that, when they turned thirteen, he would take them for a special lunch to the restaurant they had heard so much about. Jessica couldn't help but feel excitement about today's lunch date, and to find out if her father was telling her the truth about their apartment building.

Gazing up at the flags hanging in the lobby was something Jessica loved to do, as she would make up stories in her mind that she was from another country. She imagined herself a young Jewish girl from Israel hiding with her family from Roman soldiers hundreds of years ago. "Jessica!" her mother called. She startled and didn't realize she was daydreaming.

"Jessica!" her mother called again exasperated. She was already across the room. "We have to get in line."

"All right, I'm coming," Jessica called back and made her way through the crowd of people toward her mother. While she didn't have much height on her two daughters, Lisa Bianchi was one of the strongest women Jessica knew. She could tackle any challenge with determination and the Bible. Jessica always admired how her mother never seemed to be afraid of anything, and she hoped that she would be just like her someday.

As Jessica wove her way through the people, she marveled at how crowded it was for a Monday. She wasn't used to being here during the school week. However, one of the special things about her birthday this year was that her parents promised her lunch on her actual birthday, so Jessica not only had the chance to eat at the Windows on the World restaurant, but she missed a day of school as well. While she was excited, she also was hesitant. She loved her new school.

For her entire elementary school career, Jessica attended Cornerstone School, a private Christian school that included grades kindergarten through twelfth. However, for seventh grade, Jessica's parents had been persuaded to permit her to apply to LMAS, or Lower Manhattan Art School, after an extensive conference with Jessica's former principal and art teacher. When she was accepted, there was no need for discussion. The only thing Jessica regretted was not being with her life-long best friend, Samantha.

The school was only about a block and a half farther away from Cornerstone, but much more beautiful in Jessica's eyes. The old building was situated right next to a small park, and some of the classrooms had large windows with a direct view down West Broadway, ending with the World Trade Center. The building itself was an old brown brick building that stood seven stories high with beautiful, intricately carved open windows on top. To Jessica, it looked like part of an old castle.

As she reached her mother's side, Jessica felt the excitement begin to rise inside her. Even though she had been up to the observation deck at least once a year since she could remember, the excitement never grew old. After being pushed and shoved into an elevator, Jessica and her mother were finally on their way up.

CHAPTER 3

"Mom, I can see the Empire State Building today!" Jessica excitedly whispered. Sometimes the smog would cause such a cloud over New York that Jessica wasn't able to see her second favorite landmark in the city (second only to the World Trade Center).

"Yes, there it is. Did you know it was built in 1931 and used to be the tallest building in the world? It was the tallest building in New York before One World Trade Center was built in 1972."

Jessica nodded to her mother and rolled her eyes with a smile. Mrs. Bianchi loved history and never let a moment go when she could squeeze in a history lesson. Of course, this one Jessica heard every time they went up. She looked for her apartment building but couldn't see it. This made her question the authenticity of her father's stories.

She always thought about God when she was up here looking out over the city. Is this what He saw when He looked down? She learned in Sunday school that He sees everything, and her mother had reminded her often that He is everywhere and lives inside us. So what did He see when He looked down? She glanced down at the streets far below her, watching the people moving around. They reminded her of ants searching for food. Everyone had a purpose, knew exactly where they were going, and seemed to be in such a hurry to get there. A woman's voice interrupted her thoughts as a little boy almost knocked her over while he ran to get away from his mother. Jessica just smiled. Nothing was going to spoil her day today.

"All set?" her mother asked her a few minutes later.

"Yep, let's go," Jessica agreed. She didn't want to keep her father waiting; although, a small part of her thought he might have to cancel for work-related reasons anyway. Normally, he wasn't able to take a lunch break every day, and she knew he rearranged his schedule to be able to have enough time for her. She didn't want to be the cause of making him wait.

~

"Where is he?" Jessica asked anxiously, almost annoyed, as she tried peering over the tops of heads. They were waiting outside Tower 2 looking across Liberty Street toward his building. Jessica tried not to look at all the different people. Living in New York, she was taught at a very young age about diversity but still found it difficult not to stare.

"Don't stare," her mother chided her as if reading her thoughts. She couldn't help it. Her mother caught her just as she caught a glimpse of dozens of gold and silver hoops and studs attached to a boy and girl. It was difficult to look away when they walked directly in front of her. Jessica wondered how they ate without sticking themselves.

"Maybe he decided to ditch us for someone more important." The words were uttered under her breath but loud enough for her mother to hear. Before she could reprimand her daughter, however, Jessica spoke again. "There he is!" Startled at her relief, Jessica finally saw her father, his dark skin and salt and pepper hair, towering over most of the crowd of people. His six-foot-four-inch frame came quickly toward them. Her father had once been very athletic, as the pictures told her, and while he didn't have much time for sports anymore, she could still feel the muscular build as he folded his arms around her for a huge hug.

"Hey, Peanut! Happy Birthday!" he said, and released her to kiss her mother. "Peanut" was her father's nickname for her, although Jessica felt she was much too old for a nickname anymore, especially that one. She was born early and had always been on the smaller side. When she was younger, her father gave her the name and it stuck. People who didn't know them would always ask if she and Ashley were twins.

Size, though, was where the similarities between the two girls ended. Ashley had her father's Italian olive skin and green eyes, and Jessica had more of her mother's fair skin and blue eyes. Both girls had thick hair that was slightly wavy, but while Ashley's was dark brown, Jessica's was dirty blonde. Jessica always felt like she had a good blend of both her parents as she had her mother's looks and her father's spirit.

"Thanks, Dad," Jessica said with a grin. Nothing was going to ruin this day for her, even her father's need to hold on to the past.

"Are you ready for a boring afternoon surrounded by lots of serious business people eating mediocre food?"

Jessica couldn't resist giggling at her father's comment. Mr. Bianchi had a way of making her laugh with his jokes, even when she was furious at him. "Dad, if it was so boring and the food was so terrible, you wouldn't bring your clients and there wouldn't always be such a long wait."

Mr. Bianchi stifled a giggle himself as he continued the charade. "The only reason I bring people there is for the view, and by the time the salad arrives, most of them are usually tired of looking out all those gigantic windows down at the city and they are ready to leave."

Jessica was anxious to not miss their reservation, so she pulled her father's hand as they crossed the street and wove their way through the people back toward the Twin Towers. As they ascended in the elevator, Jessica watched each floor light up as they stopped to allow more people to push in. She could hardly contain her excitement. Her ears popped as they climbed higher, but she barely noticed as she smoothed the new skirt her mother had bought for her and checked to make sure she had both earrings in. The moment she had been waiting for had finally arrived!

CHAPTER 4

As the elevator doors opened, it appeared as though a flock of birds was fleeing from an overstuffed cage. Everyone poured out, and Jessica saw brilliance of light at the end of the hallway. Mr. Bianchi bent down and whispered in her ear, "Peanut, the sparkle of excitement in your eyes is almost enough to light this entire hallway." Ignoring the nickname, she instead focused on settling the stirring inside her.

Mr. Bianchi led his wife and firstborn daughter through the doorway and up to the front desk to give their name. Jessica's heart felt like it grew wings and was ready to mount. Looking around the grand room, the first thing to catch her eye was the floor-to-ceiling windows bordering the perimeter of the room. It almost seemed like there was nothing separating them from the birds in the sky. She longed to have a table beside one.

As she turned back to the front desk, she admired the beautiful screen behind the desk. She recognized it immediately. It was created by Milton Glaser, one of her favorite artists. She had done her research about the restaurant and learned that Milton Glaser designed the menus, plates, cups, and saucers, as well as the fascinating artwork on the wall. The theme seemed to be a rising sun with large rays radiating from it. It was all so very vibrant and bold. She loved it!

The maître d' led them through the tables and along the side that faced New York Harbor. Jessica noticed the crystal railings and reached out delicately to touch one. Arriving at their table, she noticed it was along the windows overlooking the city. Jessica slid into the soft bench on one side of the table while her mother sat in the chair her father held out for her, directly across Jessica next to the windows. Mr. Bianchi took the seat next to his wife.

"So, what do you think?" he asked of both his daughter and wife. Mrs. Bianchi had been to the restaurant before, but only once, the night Mr. Bianchi proposed to her. She had forgotten how marvelous it was.

"Oh, Dad," Jessica breathed. "It's the best birthday present ever!" She exhaled, trying to keep her excitement under control. After all, in her eyes, she was in one of the most prestigious restaurants in the world.

"I give Mr. Baum a lot of credit for creating something so wonderful," Mrs. Bianchi proclaimed. "Jessica, did you know—" But before she had a chance to finish, Jessica interrupted. She knew another lesson was coming.

"Did I know that Joe Baum created this restaurant? Yes, I did. I also know that he created the Four Seasons and Tavern on the Green as well. And did you know that he began having the waitstaff introduce themselves by their first name to make fine dining a little less formal? Not to mention he introduced flaming dishes to the menu." Jessica beamed at her mother.

"Well, I'm very impressed, but I'd appreciate it if you didn't interrupt me," her mother lightly scolded.

"Sorry, Mom, you've just taught me so well." Jessica smiled, as she opened her menu. "Did *you* know that Milton Glaser attended Cooper Union Art School, and he studied in Italy?" Jessica loved her art history class, and she especially loved her teacher, Mrs. West.

"Wow, I'm impressed!" Mr. Bianchi announced. "Did you learn that from Mrs. West?"

Jessica smiled. "Yes. I love that class. If I could just take art classes all day, I think I would."

"Good afternoon, my name is David. May I offer you something to drink?" A tall, twenty-something blonde interrupted the Bianchis. "And may I recommend the view. There's nothing like the Manhattan Skyline," he said and pointed across the table out the window.

Jessica glanced at her mother with a "told you," grin as the server introduced himself by his first name. Then she caught a really good look at him again and felt butterflies start fluttering in her stomach. "Hi, David, my name's Jessica. It's my birthday, and I have never been here, even though my father has eaten here hundreds of times. Did you know the art—."

"We'll have three Shirley Temples, please, David, and thank you," her father interrupted, as he ordered Jessica's favorite drink for all of them.

As David walked away, Jessica caught her father's look that told her she was not in the local diner, and to "guard her tongue" as her mother called it. Jessica felt like she was always trying to guard her tongue. She loved to meet people and, unlike her sister, was not very shy when it came to talking to strangers. Even though her mother had often scolded Jessica for talking out of turn, she knew she still had a lot of work to do.

"Okay, Dad, so where is our apartment?" Changing the conversation, Jessica could hardly wait to test him. She still thought he had been teasing her all those nights, but when Mr. Bianchi pointed to an old, finely crafted building that now housed apartments above a shop, four blocks away on Warren Street, Jessica recognized the garden decorations on the roof. The building was only partially visible from where they sat, but Jessica knew that was it. And somehow deep inside, she felt better knowing that her father could see their home those nights he was out. Even though he wasn't there physically, he could be there in spirit. Maybe he did still care about her as much as he used to.

"So, what is good, dear?" Mrs. Bianchi looked to her husband for help with the menu. It all looked so delicious, but Jessica knew what she was going to get even before walking in. She loved seafood, and her father always raved about the lobster.

"It's all delicious, but the lobster dish and herring with dilled mustard are my favorites."

"What's 'coat de buff'?" Jessica never claimed to be a French expert, even though she was part French. She looked up from her menu, expecting a response from her mother.

"It's Cote de boeuf, dear," Mrs. Bianchi said with a French accent, bringing out her heritage. "It's a thick, juicy steak."

"I think I'll go with my first choice," Jessica replied.

Her parents began to talk about grown-up stuff, so Jessica looked around the room taking in every minute detail she could about that exact moment. There were your usual guests: elderly couples, the businessmen trying to impress clients, a group of women all dressed up who probably hadn't seen each other in years. One of them seemed to be giving her friends a history lesson on the restaurant, so Jessica assumed she had been there before and didn't have any problems letting it show. At the table next to theirs, behind her parents, sat a young couple holding hands talking quietly. The girl laughed at something the boy said and quickly put her hand over her mouth as she glanced around the room to make sure she didn't interrupt anyone else's meal. Jessica wished one day *she* could come here with someone special.

She turned back to the window. Something about it just held her gaze, and she couldn't bring herself to focus on her parents. She felt like she was in another world until David came to take their orders.

∽

After lunch was finished, Jessica sat back on her bench completely satisfied with her lobster meal and looked out over New York. David brought her parents some coffee and leaned over near Jessica. "Amazing, isn't it?"

She again felt the fluttering in her stomach at the smile he sent her way and awkwardly managed a "yeah." She quickly turned her attention back to the window and scolded herself silently for being so ridiculous. But all through lunch, she couldn't help but notice the way

David stood tall in his uniform, like a soldier, and how his blue eyes stood out against his slightly darker skin.

Shaking her head to bring her thoughts back into reality, she focused her attention on the view again. She imagined herself a bird, soaring freely over this great city, looking down on the tiny dots of people and cars.

"Dad, is that your building?" she asked, pointing to a tall building not too far away.

"Yes, and if you count down five levels and to the right three windows, that's my office."

"Wow, you have that view every day from your office? How do you get any work done?"

"Easy. My back is to the window all day."

"If I worked in a building like that, I don't think I would be able to get one ounce of work done. I think I'd be daydreaming all day, watching people and wondering where they were going and who they were with."

"Ha-ha, I doubt that. I think you'd be getting a lot of work done. You'd be painting or drawing what you saw."

Her father had a point. Jessica loved taking her sketchbook to Washington Market Park where she would spend hours drawing kids playing on the playgrounds or newlyweds enjoying a picnic lunch in City Hall Park after a small ceremony inside city hall. She would have brought her sketchbook to the restaurant today except her mother forbade it. Jessica closed her eyes and took a mental picture of the view so she could remember what to draw when she got home.

~

"For some reason, I can picture you talking to the waiter like that." Ashley laughed later that same evening. They were both lying on Jessica's bed, Ashley hanging onto every word Jessica told her about her lunch. "I can't wait till it's my turn. The way you and Dad talk about it, it seems unreal."

"It does seem surreal. Like it was just a dream, and I don't want to wake up. And by the way, it's not like I said anything bad to him. He was just so cute, and I was so excited. David Fried." Jessica replayed his name over again. "Jessica Fried. That sounds so ridiculous!"

Once the girls had settled down from laughing over Jessica's last statement, Ashley began dreaming again. "Well, when I go, I want to sit by a window overlooking the water, and I won't be talking to any boys I don't know." This last comment caused Jessica to laugh out loud. "Well, good, I wouldn't want you stealing my crushes."

As the girls were laughing over their conversation, Mrs. Bianchi knocked on the door and peeked in. "Am I missing out on some secret joke?"

The girls laughed and filled their mother in on David. After they were through, Mrs. Bianci added, "I agree, he was quite a dish. I'm not sure which view was better for you, the one looking out the window or the one inside the restaurant."

"Mom! You're dating yourself again." Jessica laughed. The three girls continued their conversation until Mrs. Bianchi announced she had a cake to frost and asked her daughters to set the table for dinner.

~

Later that night, as Jessica lay in bed, she reached for the new sketchbook and pencils she received for her birthday and sketched her memories from the day's events. Tomorrow, after school, she would go to City Hall Park and find her favorite spot, leaning against a large tree trunk with a good view of city hall. She was mildly disappointed in the lack of time she had today. By the time they finished lunch and she and her mother walked home, it wasn't long before Ashley got home from school and the afternoon lessons began. Ashley was in fifth grade and one of the top musicians in her school. She took private violin lessons on Mondays while Jessica had her art class.

Jessica lightly sketched the World Trade Center, North Tower, as it looked from Church Street coming in. She drew the tall buildings that seemed so small to her from the window at the restaurant, and she made sure to highlight her apartment building with the detailed garden on the roof. Then she added an eagle, soaring high above the tower. Of course, this added another layer to the sketch since this was not a common sighting in New York City. However, Jessica thought it completed her drawing.

Birds of varying species have competed for attention as part of the Manhattan Skyline, but the story of the eagle in the Bible is one that always fascinated Jessica ever since she was a young girl. The book of Isaiah reveals that when a storm is near, the eagle doesn't seek shelter or run around in chaos. Instead, the eagle mounts up closer to God. It rises above the storm, floating higher and higher on the wind.

As she closed her eyes to relive the day, she saw David's face smiling down at them, and she quickly flipped the page and drew his face and body, standing tall even while bent slightly forward with one arm behind his back and the other offering a bottle of wine to her parents. She felt her heart soar once more as she drew his eyes. Tiny crystals that permeated his ice blue eyes. Smiling, content with her drawing, Jessica turned then to play with another gift.

Each year, Mr. and Mrs. Bianchi gave the girls one large gift and a couple smaller ones. The girls often asked for the latest "toy" that all their friends were getting (or so it seemed to them), but the response they got was always the same. "Put it on your birthday list," or "Just because everyone else has one doesn't mean you need one too." The girls knew their parents could afford to give them whatever they wanted, and when they were younger, they couldn't understand why they never got the latest game or toy as soon as it came out. Their parents repeatedly told them that just because they were blessed financially didn't mean they could have whatever they wanted when they wanted it. As Jessica grew, she learned to understand what her parents were talking about.

In fact, Jessica had grown to love the days when her mother took her to a local soup kitchen where she could volunteer her time helping to serve others. They went every other Saturday morning, and Jessica never tired from the feeling of contentment she had when a thank-you was directed her way. She knew how fortunate she was, and it gave her such joy when she took some of her allowance and passed it on to help the needy.

But now, on her thirteenth birthday, Jessica was given a gift she had so desperately wanted—a cell phone. So many of Jessica's peers already had a cell phone, and every other week, Jessica would make the argument why she needed one: "My school is farther away now. I might have an emergency on my way," or "What if I get home one day and you had to go out and I can't get into our apartment?" Whatever her argument, her parents always had a reply.

Not anymore. She knew much of this was her mother's doing. Her father frequently expressed his displeasure with the younger generation and how they were given everything at their fingertips. He called it "entitlement." Jessica knew Mrs. Bianchi agreed with her husband to an extent, but she also knew her mother was more aware of what was happening around them.

As Jessica played with her new gift, she made a mental note to thank her mother again tomorrow for convincing her father to get her a phone. A big yawn reminded Jessica that she had school tomorrow, so reluctantly she put her phone on the charger and turned out the lamp on her nightstand, rolling over to say her prayers and go to sleep.

CHAPTER 5

Six-thirty came way too soon as Jessica slammed her hand down in the direction of her nightstand, hoping eventually to find the snooze button without needing to open her eyes. She had a restless sleep after difficulty falling asleep. Visions of her birthday pushed themselves to the front of her thoughts. First and foremost was relief that her father kept his date with her, anticipation and excitement of lunch, and David causing her heart to escape from her chest. All this followed by the evening festivities.

As she stretched while trying to open her eyes, she planned her day. Today she would go to the park after school to draw. She had all these images in her mind from the previous day, and she couldn't wait to get them on paper. Details of the Center, the view she had looking up in the lobby of Tower 2, her views from the observation deck. Crawling out of bed, she heard the noises of the city and smiled. Only in the city would there be the sound of car horns blaring this early in the morning. She dragged her feet over to the window and pushed aside the curtains. The first thing that caught her eye was a tiny speck of a bird flying by the top of the

World Trade Center. Jessica sighed. The World Trade Center. Rising dominantly above all else, the rising sun glistened off the glass windows. Her mother had always told the girls that nothing on this earth is permanent. She also taught them the importance of realizing God has blessed them with all they have and nothing done on earth is to man's credit. Everything done should be done for the Lord, not for man.

Jessica thought about that as she looked up at the majestic buildings. *People built that*, she thought. *People with amazing talents designed and created these buildings, that, to many, are a symbol of our nation's strength and prosperity. Even the birds are miniscule when compared to it.* But then that thought came creeping back into her mind. Something about everything you do, do it as if it's for the Lord. She couldn't remember where that verse was in the Bible, but she had heard it often from her mother. Jessica knew the trust that so many people put into these buildings and what they stood for. She had to admit she also felt like that and silently prayed that God would change her heart.

The blaring of car horns honking brought her attention to the street below. The city was notorious for its fast-paced life. People in their suits briskly walked with a coffee in one hand, juggled a briefcase while talking on their cell phone to who knows who. She rolled her eyes as she thought about her father, knowing he would also be heading out the door shortly for work. Even with all the energy and busyness around her, Jessica couldn't imagine living anywhere else. To step outside into a canopy of skyscrapers made her feel protected. On a good day, she could look up and see the birds flying high above her. And today was definitely a good day. She loved the city. It was her home. She found comfort in knowing she could close her eyes and still find her way to her favorite snack shop, Tribeca's Tasties, on Church Street.

Jessica jumped as her thoughts were interrupted by a startling buzzing noise. What was that? *Oh, duh*, she thought. She hadn't turned her alarm clock off before getting out of bed. She ran over to it and quickly shut it off before Ashley woke up. Somehow Ashley managed to get herself dressed and ready in half the time it took her. She knew her sister would wake soon, so she quickly made her way into the one bathroom they shared before any arguments over the sink could begin.

As she made her way down the hall, Jessica overheard her parents in the kitchen discussing summer plans for the family. Every summer, the entire family went on vacation for two weeks. Usually they went to some island far away to swim and snorkel in the blue Caribbean ocean. Jessica knew what they were talking about almost immediately. For the past few years, Mrs. Bianchi had wanted to fly her parents out to the city for a visit. Paul and Marie Bauer, Jessica's grandparents, or Mémé and Papa, lived in Durango, Colorado. Jessica hadn't seen her grandparents since she was eight years old. Her parents had flown them out to New York to spend Christmas with her family after losing their youngest son, Jessica's uncle, in a car accident.

Since then, Jessica's mother had flown out to see them a few more times, but the girls couldn't miss school so they stayed home. Jessica once asked why they didn't come out more often. Her parents explained that since her grandparents lived on a ranch, it was very difficult to find someone dependable to care for things for an extended period of time.

As she closed the bathroom door, however, she overheard her mother say, "Since my parents have hired George, let's invite them out this summer."

"I'm not so sure the summer is the best time with the heat and the stuffy air. How about inviting them in the fall? Or at Christmastime?"

"Oh, that's true. I don't want to wait long though. Can we do the fall?"

Jessica couldn't remember much about her grandparents other than they went to church a lot. They lived on a large farm, and her grandfather liked to tell stories about his horse, Rocket. This year, Jessica secretly hoped her mother's wish would come true.

She left the bathroom and stopped in the kitchen to put in her thoughts before she went to get dressed. "I hope nothing keeps them this year from coming. I'd love to see them again. I barely remember Mémé and Papa."

"I hope so too, honey. In fact, I know it. We will get them out here before this year is over. I'm going to call Mémé as soon as I know she's up." And with that, Mrs. Bianchi smiled at her daughter and reached for her coffee.

Jessica stared at her mother in disbelief. She doubted they would be able to come. Something always seemed to come up when her parents had asked. She thought about her mother. Mrs. Bianchi had such a positive attitude. She called it "keeping the faith." Jessica called it wishful thinking, but she kept that to herself. Her mother seemed convinced, so she didn't want to be the one to spoil it for her.

CHAPTER 6

Jessica loved her walk to school, especially in the springtime. The morning air was still cool enough for a windbreaker, but the sun was shining down, casting shadows from the buildings. Jessica turned her head to get a good look of the World Trade Center as she waited on the corner of Warren and Church. Samantha's apartment building was also on Warren Street but toward West Broadway. Since both girls had to walk up Church Street for school, they met every morning on the corner to walk together. Jessica usually arrived to school a little early, but that was fine with her. It gave her time to sketch. The memories from yesterday were still so vivid in her mind that she was actually looking forward to any free time she could get.

Jessica leaned against a street sign and looked down her block into City Hall Park. She often thought about what she would be when she grew up, if she would be like one of those ladies she watched, clicking their high heels on the sidewalk. Jessica had mixed feelings when it came to what she wanted to be. Part of her wanted to teach art in a school or stay home and be a wife and a mother like her mom. But there was also a small part of her that wanted to be like those women, and work in the World Trade Center with an office near the top so she could sit at her desk and look out her large picture window every day.

"Hi, Jessi! What's so interesting about city hall?" Jessica didn't even hear Sami approaching. One of the first things the two girls did when they became best friends was to come up with matching nicknames for each other, making them seem more like sisters.

Matching Sami's step, Jessica countered, "Nothing. Other than it's one of the most beautiful old buildings in Manhattan."

Sami rolled her eyes. "Maybe to you, but give me the New York Public Library any day." Jessica laughed. Even though she and Sami had similar interests, like ordering the same exact snack at Tribeca's Tasties, they had lots of different interests too and loved that about their friendship.

"Absolutely, you can have the library. I wouldn't know how to find anything in there anyway!"

"That's why you have me—to help you learn your ABCs! So before this conversation continues to go nowhere, what did you get for your birthday, and how was your father at lunch?" Jessi and Sami told each other everything, so Sami was aware of the strained relationship between her best friend and her father.

As Jessica began telling Sami about her phone, she watched as Sami's eyes widened. Sami was one of the few people Jessica knew who also did not have her own cell phone. Her parents held very similar beliefs as Jessica's, and the girls always believed that was part of the reason they got along so well. Not to mention that both of their moms were in the same child-birthing class and attended the same church.

"But you know what? As much as I loved getting the phone, I think I almost loved the lunch more. Putting aside all the glitz and glamour, I felt like I was on top of the world, sitting up there eating that food, drinking out of that crystal. Not only that, but my father actually stayed the entire time and we talked. It was almost like old times."

"Well, it is called Windows on the *World*, you know." Sami was always one waiting for any opportunity to comment or make a joke. "And if your father skipped out on your birthday lunch, I don't think he'd ever hear the end of it from your mother. But in all honesty, I'm glad it was good."

"Thanks. Me too. But seriously, I really felt like I was on top of the world. Down here, it's like we're just little ants, always working, always moving. But up there, it just seemed so peaceful and surreal. Like all the little things in life didn't matter. I can't wait to go back." And with that, their conversation wrapped up with the last few details revolving around David.

"How would you compare him to Ben Miller?" Sami's eyes twinkled as she asked this last question.

"Sami, shhhh!" Jessica quickly glanced around, making sure none of her classmates were nearby to hear their conversation.

Ben Miller was a boy Jessica met in the fall during orientation. He was the first boy she ever had a crush on. Jessica remembered the first time she saw him. She couldn't seem to take her eyes off his dazzling green eyes and dark hair. The way he flicked his head to get the hair out of his face made her stomach flip flop again just thinking about it.

"So? You didn't answer my question. Are you just going to have that goofy grin on your face and let yourself get hit by a car? Or are you going to tell me whose face is going through that brain of yours right now?"

As they finished crossing over West Broadway, heading down Reade Street, Jessica thought how Sami really had a gift of patience. "He was just as cute but in a different way. No, he wasn't cute. He was so, I don't know, grown-up looking. He was handsome. He had big muscles and facial hair!"

At that they both laughed, and after a quick hug good-bye, Sami continued on past Hudson Street to finish her short walk to Cornerstone while Jessica turned and headed up Hudson, daydreaming about two very different boys fighting for room in her thoughts.

CHAPTER 7

The last few months of school wrapped up quickly with Ashley's concert and the LMAS annual art show the last week in May. It was a time for the students to show off their hard work to their families. Jessica won a ribbon for most realistic sketch, which was a view of the city from Windows on the World restaurant. Ben picked her out of the crowd that night to congratulate her. She had done a pretty good job of keeping her distance from him for most of the spring, mostly because she was afraid her mouth would have a mind of its own if she ran into him. That night, however, she was speechless when he spoke to her. She managed a weak "thanks" and somehow got through introductions with her family and Sami, who was there to support her best friend.

Studying for finals kept Jessica busy enough not to notice how often her father was working. School ended with all her final exams aced, and Jessica was finally ready for summer vacation to start. It was the first night of vacation. Jessica had just walked in the door after celebrating the end of school over a Tribeca sundae with her friends when she heard her parents talking in the kitchen. She popped in with the intention of saying a quick hello before changing into her shorts and crashing on the sofa to watch whatever old movie was on TV that night.

"Are you sure you heard right, Anthony? I mean, maybe Rick heard wrong?"

Jessica peered around the corner, careful so as to not disturb her parents' conversation. Rick Shelton was a good friend of her father's, and they worked together.

Anthony Bianchi shook his head. "I know it's something to question as it's only a rumor. But his brother-in-law works in DC and that's what he said. There was a terrorist threat today involving Al-Qaeda attacks, and that hasn't been the first. What is it going to take for our government to realize that our country is not invincible? I think we should stay put this summer."

Jessica leaned back against the doorframe and had to put her hands over her mouth to keep from letting a gasp escape. Terrorism. That word scared her beyond her imagination. She didn't know who Al-Qaeda was, but she always believed in the safety of the country and assumed nothing could happen to it. Just then the realization hit her that she was just like the people in the government offices her father was talking about.

"Why don't we pray for our country and our leaders, specifically President Bush, for wisdom and guidance?"

Jessica couldn't believe her mother. Even during times of potential crisis, her first thought went to prayer. She couldn't take it any longer.

"Why are you so calm? Didn't you hear Dad? Terrorist attacks are making us cancel our summer vacation!"

Her parents' faces showed the shock of having been overheard. It was her father who spoke first, "First of all, young lady, don't ever speak to your mother like that again. Second, it is very rude to listen in on other people's conversations whether you intended to or not. Now you owe your mother an apology."

Jessica could see by her father's expression that she was in trouble, but she didn't really care. She took a deep breath to calm herself before speaking, "I'm sorry, Mom. I just don't understand."

Mrs. Bianchi rose from her chair and went to put her arms around her daughter. At the sound of her father's raised voice, Ashley came out of her room and both girls stood in the kitchen doorway afraid to cross any line with their father.

"Come, sit down, I want to share something with you." As the girls hesitantly sat down between both parents, Mrs. Bianchi looked from one daughter to the other before beginning, "When I was fifteen, I was away at a summer camp about two hours from my home. My parents both came to know the Lord when I was about twelve. They tried to teach me about Jesus and His love for me, but it was easier to raise my brothers in it since they were only one at the time. That's all they knew growing up. I knew in my head Jesus died for me, but the rebellious spirit inside me refused to want His help. I believed I could do all things on my own, and I was the only one who controlled my future. Because of this, I would get angry anytime someone didn't do what I thought they should have done. I was always feeling very uptight and critical of others. Of course, at the time, I thought I was happy. Only much later did I realize how much turmoil was going on inside.

"So the summer I was fifteen, my parents thought it would be a good idea to send me to a Christian camp for a couple of weeks. I had just finished a very difficult freshman high school year where my new 'friends' were offering me cigarettes while reassuring me that everyone in our class was stealing from the local convenient store. My life had become one filled with fear. I was constantly looking over my shoulder, wondering if I was being followed by a cop, or worse, my parents.

One night, after my father bailed me out of jail for stealing, I overheard them praying. I knew they always prayed for everything. I rolled my eyes as I walked by their bedroom, but then something drew me back to listen. Usually they thanked God for bringing me to Him. But that night, I heard my father through tears ask God for guidance to know how to help me. My heart began to hurt. I felt so badly that I led them to that point. After that night, I agreed to go to the camp when they brought it up to me the next morning.

"While at camp, I met some amazing people who helped me see what trusting God is really about. One night, one of the girls from the cabin next to mine told me about a secret meeting place in the woods on the other side of the lake from our camp. She said all the girls in her cabin as well as in mine have been going over there each night. They found benches in a circle around an old fire pit. She invited me to join them this particular night."

"Mom, you didn't go, did you? That sounds so scary!"

"Believe it or not, I did go, Ashley. I wanted to please these girls more than anything. And since I hadn't made many other friends, not that I was trying, I was thrilled these girls let me in on their secret. So that night, Pamela, that was her name, told me to meet them by the canoes at ten thirty. It never occurred to me to ask why I had to meet them there and not just go with them. But I went to bed fully dressed, just like the other girls, and grabbed my flashlight at ten twenty to head over to the lake.

"As I approached the meeting place, I noticed some canoes were already gone and there were lights over on the other side. I felt angry they didn't wait for me, but I was a good swimmer, so I climbed into the canoe and went to meet them.

"When I arrived on the other side, I climbed out of the canoe and with my flashlight found my way into the woods a little bit to where I thought I saw them. Instead of being greeted by the girls, however, I was greeted by all sorts of sounds, branches breaking, whispering, animals making their nightly noises, and for the first time in a long time, I felt real fear. I tried to follow their whispers but only felt myself getting more lost with each step. But then I heard Pamela come up behind me, and she encouraged me to follow her to the meeting place. Well, of course, she just led me deeper into the woods, trying to get me very confused. Then she began walking the opposite direction quickly. When I turned around to try to follow her, she was already too far away. It didn't take me long to lose her completely."

"What did you do, Mom?"

Mrs. Bianchi looked directly at Jessica and Ashley before continuing, "For the first time, I prayed with a sincere heart. After calling for Pamela and the other girls, I heard them run away laughing and realized that I had been tricked. I suddenly remembered a verse my mother used to share with me after I was in trouble with the law. It was from Micah, and the only reason I remembered that was because there was a boy named Micah at my school who was strange and different, or so I thought, back then. Anyway, that verse says, 'Do not trust in a friend; do not put your confidence in a companion.' Then later in the chapter it says, 'Therefore I will look to the Lord; I will wait for the God of my salvation; My God will hear me.'

"So I prayed harder than I had ever done before. I didn't know at the time that God could and would really speak to me, so I wasn't sure where that verse came from in my memory. But I began saying it over and over, especially the last part, about waiting for God and that He will hear me. I continued to cry out to God and I began to feel a peace inside me that I had never felt before. Then I remembered Psalm 91, about how God will protect us from even the worst situations if we set our love upon Him."

"How did you remember Psalm 91?" Jessica wondered.

"Because just like I read it to you every morning before you leave for school, my mother used to read it to us each morning. It stuck in my brain, and I found it when I needed it most."

A newfound knowledge of Mrs. Bianchi's relation-ship with God began to dawn on Jessica, and she found herself thinking about all the verses her mother read to her when she needed them.

"So what happened?" Ashley interjected her sister's thoughts.

"Then I sat down."

"What?" Both girls thought they misunderstood their mother.

"I sat down. Right there in the dark woods. After I had repented and turned back to God, I felt such a peace, I decided to sit down and wait for help even if it wasn't going to come until morning. It turned out I didn't have to wait long, because after only a few minutes of sitting, I heard adult voices and saw flashlights nearby. Apparently one of the girls from the other cabin, who was not in on the prank, overheard the others talking about it when they returned, and she went to tell our counselor."

"Wow, Mom, I never knew you went through stuff like that," Ashley commented. "I get it! Because Psalm 91 tells us that even if thousands fall at our side, no harm will come on us if we trust in God! *That's* why you were so calm when you were talking to Dad."

Mrs. Bianchi looked over at her husband, and they exchanged knowing smiles. "That's exactly right, honey. Because I know that no matter what happens around us, God will cover us with His wings."

Jessica listened intently to her family, all the while wishing she could feel the same peace her mother felt.

CHAPTER 8

July came and went without any more news on terrorist attacks, which relieved Jessica greatly. It took her a couple of weeks to stop thinking about that conversation, but eventually, her fears subsided and life went back to normal. She spent her mornings at City Hall Park drawing, and her afternoons often at Tribeca's Tasties with her friends. When she and Ashley could drag their mother away from her quilting, the three girls would go down to the World Trade Center and have lunch at the mall.

It was during one of these visits, on a particularly hot afternoon in August, that Mrs. Bianchi's cell phone rang. The three of them were enjoying a relaxing afternoon in the courtyard surrounded by the towers. The girls were on the stone wall while Mrs. Bianchi sat on a bench just below them. Ashley was still finishing her frozen yogurt. Jessica had just finished hers and was casually glancing around the courtyard in hopes of catching a glimpse of David again. She was laying in her favorite spot on the wall, close enough to the shade of a tree but still able to access a clear view of the "Sphere" by Fritz Koenig. She didn't know anything about it, but being an artist, she loved the design and the way the sun glinted off the gold. While she reached for her colored pencils and sketchbook to capture the view, Ashley grabbed her Claire's bag and began removing her new earrings from the cardboard display. Jessica and Ashley exchanged glances as they heard their mother say, "That would be perfect, Mom. The weather will hopefully be a little cooler by then." After a few more pleasantries, their mother remarked how much she was looking forward to seeing "you both" before she hung up.

Mrs. Bianchi pointed out something about the way the sun shone, but the two sisters became quickly exasperated and began to press their mother about her conversation: "Was that Mémé?" "What were you talking about?" "Are they coming?"

Mrs. Bianchi laughed as she held up her hands in surrender to her girls. "All right, all right, I'll tell you. It was going to be a surprise, but Mémé and Papa are flying out here for a week or two next month. Things have settled down for your father at work, and he thought this would be a good time before they get hectic again."

The girls couldn't believe their ears. "Really, they're really coming this time?"

"They are *really* coming this time," said Mrs. Bianchi, repeating her daughter's words. "Now let's finish up our shopping. We've only a week left before school begins, and your grandparents are hopefully flying out on Monday, September 10, if they can get a flight. All of a sudden, I have a lot to do." And with that, Mrs. Bianchi began walking toward the mall, leaving the girls still stunned over her brief description of what they considered the biggest event of the year, if not the decade!

CHAPTER 9

Jessica was sitting at Tribeca's Tasties enjoying her last day of summer vacation with a couple of friends, discussing the upcoming visit of her grandparents. The entire household was in a whirlwind as Mrs. Bianchi was preoccupied with planning all the things they would do together during the visit. Jessica was just explaining the latest discussion her parents were having about going to New Jersey for a day to visit her father's parents when she noticed out of the corner of her eye the door open. Jessica glanced over and her stomach flip-flopped as Ben and some friends entered. Jessica could see he was laughing about something. He saw her immediately, and he stopped at their table to say hi before heading to the counter to order. Jessica, not one to be shy, quickly stuffed a gigantic bite of her caramel cheesecake into her mouth and just smiled and waved.

"Hi, guys," Ben said as he put his hands in his pockets. The rest of the girls said hi, but Jessica just waved and smiled.

After he walked away and approached the counter, Sami elbowed Jessica. "Why didn't you say anything?"

"I had food in my mouth. I didn't want to act rudely and speak when I had my mouth full."

"Seems to me," Emily Wilson, a good friend of Jessica's who she'd met at LMAS, commented, "that you did it on purpose."

"Jessica Bianchi, in all my life I have never known you to keep your mouth shut. And I definitely have never known you to be one who has nothing to say. So why did you do it?" Sami prodded her good friend who began to blush.

"That's why I did it," Jessica replied. Both Sami and Emily exchanged curious glances before Jessica was pressed to continue. "I always have something to say even if it's not the appropriate thing. I was afraid I'd say something that would completely embarrass me. Ben is so nice and he always seems to say just the right thing at just the right time. I'm the complete opposite! He's the one person I don't want to see my true colors! So can we please forget about him and enjoy the rest of our summer?" And, with that, Jessica stuffed another forkful into her mouth, and the trio shared a good laugh.

CHAPTER 10

As it turned out, Jessica saw much more of Ben than she had hoped once school started. The bell rang for first period to begin, and as Jessica was just settling in to a desk in the second row, Ben burst through the door out of breath. Jessica wanted to wave and call out his name at the same time she wanted to shrink so low she was hiding under her desk so he wouldn't see her. She decided to do neither. Instead, she quickly scooped up her sketchbook and bent over to tuck it into her bag.

As she was sitting up, she casually glanced behind her and caught Ben smiling at her from the next aisle, one row back. She flushed and smiled with a quick wave before turning back to the front of the room where her math teacher was just beginning the lesson.

The rest of the day went by quickly, and at lunch, Jessica was able to find Emily. They gave each other a big hug and laughed as they competed to tell each other about their first day so far. The girls were pleased to find out they had two classes together in the afternoon, remaining inseparable until last period when they went their separate ways and made plans to meet for lunch the next day.

~

That night, once again, the two Bianchi girls were sprawled across Jessica's bed recalling the events of their day to their mother who sat in a chair leaning against the desk. Ashley was just finishing up retelling a conversation that took place between her teacher and one of the Jewish boys in her Bible history class. "And then Mr. Sorgan asked Josh if he would like to present an oral report on it. Josh was so embarrassed, his face turned so red I didn't think he'd survive!"

"Well, it sounds like Mr. Sorgan seemed to believe that Josh knew enough about the topic that he could teach the rest of the class something. That's quite a compliment."

Jessica smiled to herself as she watched her mother. Mrs. Bianchi always seemed to know just what to say in a calm, caring way. Not for the first time, Jessica took a look on the inside and hoped that someday she would be just like her.

"Speaking of Jewish boys, Jess, did you see Ben today?" Jessica was brought back to the moment by the question her sister posed.

She looked over at her mother who was smiling at her. "Actually," she sighed, "I did see him today. And I will be seeing him for the rest of the year. He is in almost all of my classes."

"Ooooh, I guess you won't be missing many days of school this year then," her sister teased.

"If I had my way, we wouldn't have any classes together. Me and my big mouth are gonna have to have a talk this year before I say something I completely regret. This is going to be one long year. But enough about Ben. Mom, how are plans coming for Mémé and Papa's trip here?"

"Everything is just about settled. They will land at one thirty next Monday afternoon at JFK Airport. Your father and I will meet them when they land, and hopefully we'll be home before you two. Mémé and I have talked about some of the sights they want to see while they're here, and one of the first things we plan to do is drive over to New Jersey to see Nana and Nonno since it's been ages since they've seen each other."

Jessica and Ashley both cried out to go with them as they loved visiting their grandparents on their father's side, but Mrs. Bianchi was firm. "You two will have school that day, and since it's only going to be your first full week of school for the year, I'm not willing to pull you out yet. Besides, Nana and Nonno said they would come for the day one Saturday to visit while Mémé and Papa are here, and we can all go down to the WTC for lunch." The girls seemed satisfied with that, although they loved going to Bloomfield, where their grandparents lived.

CHAPTER 11

Monday, September 10, approached before anyone was ready. Excitement filled the entire apartment as Jessica was getting her bag packed. The night before, she had moved her belongings into Ashley's room so their grandparents could have her room since it was larger and had a bigger bed. Ashley only had bunk beds, and the girls were already creating various ways to set up forts with blankets and furniture. Jessica took one sniff and smiled. Her mother had already begun preparations for dinner, and she was making her famous French cassoulet. Mr. Bianchi left for work before the girls were awake since he had to leave early for the airport.

"Pleeasse, can't you call the school and tell them we need to leave early so we can go with Dad to the airport?" Jessica already knew the answer since she must've asked the question at least a hundred times in the last two days.

"No and no. You will have plenty of time to spend with them after they arrive here." With that, her mother said a quick prayer, kissed the top of her forehead, and sent Jessica out the door for school.

The morning promised to be a beautiful day, and Jessica tipped her head up to catch some last rays of sunshine before the winter kept them hidden. She cast her usual glance down toward the towers, grinned as she thought about how all seemed right with the world, and started off to meet Sami.

~

Jessica typically arrived home about a half hour before Ashley since her day ended earlier. However, on this particular day, she felt the urge to wait for Ashley so they could walk home together. She called her mother to let her know, and as she waited, she tried to picture what the reunion would be like when the girls arrived home. She felt nervous and excited all at the same time. Now that she was finally going to see her grandparents, she felt a little unsure. It had been almost five years since she last saw them. As she glanced down at her frame, she considered all the growing she had done in those years, even though she wasn't much taller. She thought, *Would they recognize me? Would I recognize them? What would we talk about?* She was prepared to hear more stories about Rocket, the wonder horse, but *would they be interested in her drawings or her life? Would they have a funny smell like Sami's grandparents? Maybe, being on vacation, they would just want to sit around all day watching game shows, trying to beat the contestants as well as each other. Would they even like the city? Maybe they would hate the noise and be miserable the whole time since they were so used to the quiet of Colorado.*

It was this last thought that came and went as she saw Ashley and some friends exit the building. Ashley said something to them, and then with a quizzical look, she quickly headed over to her waiting sister.

"What's the matter, Jess? You look like you're going to pass out. Are you feeling okay? Is someone hurt?"

"I'm fine! What, can't a girl wait for her little sister once in a while without being interrogated?" Jessica snipped in a reply, and she started stomping off down the road.

Ashley was taken aback by Jessica's response, but she let it go and picked up her pace to catch her sister. "Okay, sure you can. I'm sorry, you just usually don't wait for me. Are you sure you're okay?"

"I'm sorry, I'm just a little nervous and thought if we went in the door together, it wouldn't feel as awkward."

"You, nervous?" Ashley couldn't believe what she was hearing. "You're like the boldest person I've ever known. I've never known you to be nervous about anything."

"Yeah, well, I'm nervous about seeing Mémé and Papa again. I'm just not sure how much they remember us."

Ashley comforted her sister. "You'll see. This trip will be a lot of fun. Hopefully we'll see a little more of Dad these next couple weeks, unless he decides to move into his office till they leave!"

The girls let out a laugh over that and were still joking about it when they reached their building. After exiting the elevator, Jessica paused just outside their door to say a quick prayer under her breath that God would help her relax but, more importantly, to help her remember not to say something to her grandparents she might regret. As she walked down the hall, she heard laughter and felt herself already relaxing.

"Jessica! Ashley!" The girls were greeted at the door with a great big hug as their grandmother embraced them, one at a time. "Jessica, Ashley, I can't believe how grown up you two are. You are such beautiful young ladies."

Jessica smiled and thanked her grandmother. It was Papa's turn. "Hey, now, darlin'. Come get into these arms!" Jessica silently winced as her grandfather squeezed her so tight she felt like her eyeballs would pop out.

"Hi, Papa," Jessica said.

"Girls, why don't you get your things settled and come back out here and tell us how your day was."

"Okay, Mom." Jessica was thankful for her mother's interjection. She quickly changed and unpacked her bag before settling into her favorite oversized chair across from her grandparents on the couch.

Ashley grabbed a bean bag from her room and settled into it next to the fireplace. She then was quickly whisked into a conversation with her grandfather.

"I still can't get over how much you've changed, you're so grown up. Tell me, what are you up to these days? Still drawing?" Jessica's grandmother asked.

Jessica relaxed as she looked at her and replied, "Yes, actually, I have a whole book of sketches from around the city. Would you like to see?" Jessica was hoping any reservations her grandparents had of the city would dissolve if she showed them her artwork.

"Lisa, you have quite a talented young lady here," Jessica's grandmother praised as she looked at the drawings. "I can't wait to walk around and see these images live."

"Oh, Mom, can we go now?" A brilliant idea popped into Jessica's mind. "Can we take Mémé and Papa to the mall for dinner? I know you already made it, but can we save it for tomorrow? Please?" Jessica held her breath as she waited for the response.

"Please, Mom? You kept telling us how much Mémé and Papa couldn't wait to see the city. Please, can we go?" Ashley was just as excited as her sister at this new prospect.

"We can do whatever Mémé and Papa want, although I'm sure they're tired." Mrs. Bianchi looked to her parents.

"Well, what are we waiting for? Let's go to this popular mall for some dinner," Papa said. Jessica jumped with excitement as her grandfather winked at her and stood to get ready.

The rest of the afternoon and evening continued just as Jessica hoped for the most part. As the family strolled down the street, the girls talked incessantly, filling their grandparents in on their lives in the city, and in turn, they listened to stories about Rocket, of which Jessica thoroughly enjoyed.

"Oh, they are just as majestic as I remember them." Mémé put her hand on Jessica's arm to stop her dead in her tracks. Jessica smiled, nodding in agreement. Turning onto Church Street, this was her favorite view of the towers as well. Looking at her daughter, she continued, "I don't know why we haven't managed to get here more often. I feel like I've missed so much of my granddaughters' lives."

"Don't be so hard on yourself, Mom. I know how difficult it is to get away from the ranch. It is an amazing view, though, I do agree." Mrs. Bianchi gave her mother a sideways hug and took her hand to catch up to the men who had already crossed the street before realizing they were alone.

Dinner at the mall was a quick stop at Sbarro for some pizza, and the family ate as they walked through the mall. Jessica's fears were quickly put to rest, and she thought nothing of grabbing her grandmother's hand to show her the lobby in Tower 2.

Later that night, bedtime crept up on everyone as they continued their visit in front of the fire. Even the storm that came through while they were down at dinner didn't dampen their spirits. The topic eventually turned to plans for the next day which included a visit to New Jersey.

After the girls had pushed their bedtime as far as they could, the hugs between grandparents and granddaughters were a little bit tighter than they had been a few hours before. And while everyone was hesitant to break the bonds of the day, it felt good as each member of the family settled into their beds, looking forward to the events of the following day.

CHAPTER 12

Art history, first period of Jessica's day, was her favorite class. Tuesday morning, Jessica found herself captivated by the lesson. Mrs. West was talking about the Louvre, a museum in Paris that housed some of the most famous artwork including the *Mona Lisa*. She loved learning about older pieces of art and the methods used to create them. Just as she raised her hand to ask a question, there was a loud boom outside. It sounded like a large car accident that occurred directly outside their classroom window. All the kids ran to the window to see. Mrs. West even joined them to make sure everything was okay. Jessica had an unsettled feeling in the pit of her stomach as she felt that familiar sense of fear come over her. She tried to will it away as she always did when she felt afraid, but she couldn't. As she looked out the window, she couldn't see anything. Most of Jessica's classes were on the first and second floor of the school, but one of her classes was on the third floor with a perfect view down Hudson Street and extended all the way down West Broadway to the Towers. All she looked at now, though, was another brick building. If she craned her neck to the left, she could see a few leaves from the trees in Duane Park, but she still felt something was wrong.

"What the heck was that?" Ben asked. Before Mrs. West could reply, the school alarm went off. Mrs. West instructed the class to quickly gather in the back corner of the room just the way they rehearsed the first week of school.

Jessica's heart began to pound, and she wondered if anyone else could hear it. "Mrs. West, what is going on?" She asked.

"Awww, it's probably some prank. I betcha one of those stupid seventh graders pulled the alarm."

Funny, Jessica thought, as she looked toward the sound of the voice, *we were those stupid seventh graders just a few months ago.* But it didn't surprise her when she saw who said it. Tommy Woodward, or "Tom," as he demanded he be called, was one of the biggest bullies in the school. He didn't care who he said it to, he was one of those kids who said the first thing that came to his mind when he opened his mouth. Before Jessica could respond with what she was thinking though, they heard footsteps walking quickly down the hallway.

Mrs. West was called into the hallway and came back seconds later with instructions. "Everyone, there's no need to worry, but we need to quickly move to the community room. Please walk, no running."

As Jessica began to walk, she looked over at Tom who seemed to have a panicked look in his eyes. "What do you mean there's no need to worry?" he demanded. "Then why do we have to go to the community room? That's in the basement. Why can't we stay here?"

"Tom, please don't argue with me right now. I'm just following instructions."

"How long do we have to be there? I want to get my things."

"We were instructed to leave everything, so please just follow the crowd, and hopefully, we will learn more in a few minutes." Mrs. West was one of the most patient people Jessica ever met.

Jessica was impressed by how calm Mrs. West was acting, and she wondered if Mrs. West was a Christian. Jessica knew that Christians were supposed to love everyone, even the "unlovely." Tom was definitely one of the "unlovely" ones to her. She had a hard time loving someone who was so mean to everyone else.

As Jessica approached the top of the stairwell to join other students from the top levels already on their way down, she looked up and down and suddenly felt like cattle being rounded up into one tiny space. As they made their way down a staircase at the far end of the science wing, she looked around at all the faces. Some of the kids thought this was just a drill, so they were messing around and laughing. She turned the other way and made brief eye contact with Emily who smiled and gave a quick wave before being pushed down the stairs to the left. Jessica heard some of the students say something about smoke coming from Tower 1. She felt her heart quicken and wished she could just get to a window on the south side of the building. Jessica looked down to make sure she didn't trip anyone on the stairs, and just as she reached the bottom, another loud crash came ringing through her ears. Feeling fear rise up inside her once more, she thought it would take over her body. She tried to think of a Bible verse, any verse, her parents had given her to help when she felt this way.

A seventh grade girl somewhere behind Jessica started to cry and Jessica silently prayed for help. Suddenly, she didn't know how or where it came from, but Jessica began whispering the first verse she thought of.

"God has not given us a spirit of fear, but of power, and of love, and a sound mind." She couldn't remember where it came from, but that didn't matter to her. She kept repeating it over and over again under her breath. Then something hit her about it that she had never realized before. The verse talked about how God gave us love and power while, in the same sentence, explaining that He did not give us fear. A sudden act of love and power came over Jessica, and she turned around and whispered the verse to the seventh grader behind her, who smiled briefly through her tears and thanked her.

At the bottom of the stairs, Mr. Montanez and Ms. King, the principal and vice principal, respectively, were pushing a large cart with a TV on it into a small room set off the large community room. Jessica heard excitement behind her as kids threw out their guesses as to what they were watching. "I bet they are putting a movie on for us to distract us from something we're not supposed to know about," one of her classmates was saying.

"No way, how would they get all of us into that small room? It's probably some stupid assembly. But whatever, if it gets us out of class, I'm all for it."

"You're both wrong. It's probably some reward we are getting for something we did."

Jessica thought they were all wrong, but she kept quiet. Funny, she usually had a lot to say to anyone who would listen, but not now. She wasn't sure why, but she felt the need to be silent as she looked around her, trying to take in every detail. Entering the large room, she heard a whisper regarding the World Trade Center, and her heart started to race.

CHAPTER 13

Mr. Bianchi always sat at his desk with his back to the window. He knew he would never get any work done if he stared out the window all day. In more ways than one, Jessica was a miniature of her father. She acquired her love of the city from him. He didn't know why exactly, but as a kid, he was always in awe of the big buildings of the city. From a very young age, he knew this was where he wanted to work and live. He never thought much about having a family and raising children, but that part just sort of happened. Fortunately for him, he found someone who loved it just as much as he did.

On this particular morning, Mrs. Bianchi was taking her parents to New Jersey to visit his family. He thought back to the brief argument they had that morning as he was supposed to go with them. Unfortunately, as he tried to explain to his wife, sometimes things come up and sacrifices have to be made. He promised to make it up to the family.

Placing the phone on its hook after finishing his early business call, Mr. Bianchi swiveled his chair to take a break from his work and enjoy the view across the street. He was one of the fortunate ones with a desirable view directly across from the World Trade Center plaza. Rising out of his chair, he went to the window and stared down at the people far below. Smiling as he looked up to Windows on the World Restaurant, he thought back to the special lunch date on Jessica's birthday.

"Oh, Peanut," he muttered under his breath. "So young and still so much to learn about life." Mr. Bianchi loved both his daughters equally, but there were times a sense of urgency came over him to say an extra prayer for Jessica during his day. He never knew the reason, but he knew her personality. She had a lot of spunk, and he chuckled as he thought back to some of the things he had done when he was young. She was so much like him, and a pang of guilt swept over him as he reflected on the change in their relationship. He was working more lately, and he knew it bothered Jessica. No amount of explaining was enough for her though, and he sensed her resentment building as the last twelve months or so passed. Ashley, on the other hand, was so much like their mother—sweet, quiet, and gentle; able to handle any obstacle life threw at her.

He had just finished this thought when he felt the urging again. "Lord, once again, you stop me during my busy day to pray for Jessica. Cover her with Your wings and lead her and guide her according to Your perfect plan. Direct her steps, Lord." Mr. Bianchi was just about to return to his desk when he sensed another urging, stronger this time. "Send Your angels around my entire family, Lord, as they go about their day. Cover them with the precious blood that was poured out for us."

Just as Mr. Bianchi looked up one last time to see the sun's rays shining off the towers across the street, he noticed an airplane flying low. His first thought was that someone was being funny, and they were doing a flyby, heading toward the building to make a last minute detour away. But for some reason, he couldn't take his eyes from the scene and, instead, sensed a great urgency to continue praying. Within seconds, he knew why.

CHAPTER 14

From a very young age, Jessica had been told she was observant. Watching people, she saw emotions and expressions that most kids didn't give two thoughts about. As the students were getting settled in the community room, Jessica, already seated on the floor, looked around at the adults. She glanced again at Mrs. West. Throughout this entire ordeal, she seemed nervous but remained calm. Then she looked to Mr. Montanez and wished she had a sketchbook so she could draw what she saw. She always considered Mr. Montanez a man with great personality. He could make the students laugh at the drop of a hat, and he was always getting high fives from many of the boys as they passed him in the hall. Yet he was well-respected by all the faculty and students alike. The only time Mr. Montanez was not wearing a broad smile was when he was disciplining somebody. Even then, it wasn't for very long. Today, however, looking at him this way, Jessica saw traces of fear, worry, and something that seemed almost like panic to her. It told her that whatever had happened was not just a car accident, but may be her worst fear.

"Look at that face. You'd think he's just been given a death sentence." Jessica jumped. It was like someone was reading her thoughts. She looked to her left and saw Ben sitting next to her.

As hard as she tried to appear calm and together, only one word would leave her lips. "What?"

"Mr. Monty. Anybody who knows him would know there was something seriously wrong if they took a good look at his face." Mr. Monty was a term of endearment given by the students to Mr. Montanez.

"Oh, that—I mean, yeah, I know, right?" Jessica didn't know if it was the embarrassment of being caught staring, the fear of the situation, or the nerves of sitting so close to Ben that she could smell his laundry detergent. She quickly composed herself. "Any idea what it's all about? I've never seen him like that."

"I don't know, but if you ask me, it can't be good. I heard talk of some sort of crash at Tower 1. I have a feeling we'll find out whatever it is soon though." With that, Ben pointed to the small teachers' room where many of the teachers and staff were stone-still as their eyes locked onto the TV screen in front of them. Jessica noticed some began to weep silently while others covered their mouths with their hands. She wished they were close enough to see what the screen showed and what the announcers were saying. Ben said something and pointed to the front of the room as Mr. Montanez stepped forward.

What Jessica and Ben heard, along with every other member of that school packed like sardines in the large room, was something they would never forget for as long as they lived. Mr. Montanez was trying to compose himself before speaking, "We have just received word that there has been an accident."

"An accident?" Jessica looked at Ben with questions in her eyes. He only looked back at her with the same questions.

"They are calling it 'World Trade Center Disaster.'" Mr. Montanez had to pause before continuing, "Not much is known yet, but the Twin Towers have been attacked by two airplanes. So far, that's all the information…"

Jessica could not peel her eyes from the man she saw in front of her. "Terrorist attack…on purpose…planes were hijacked…dead…" These were all parts of what was being discussed quietly by the teachers around her, but Jessica couldn't piece it all together. All she saw in her mind was the North Tower standing tall against a clear blue backdrop of a sky, when all of a sudden, an airplane came in from the side and collided smack into the building. She was just wrapping her feelings and emotions around what she imagined when she realized that must have been what the loud crash was that they heard.

.

CHAPTER 15

Anthony Bianchi had never felt real fear in all his life. Yet as he stood there praying fervently, watching the airplane collide directly in front of him into the North Tower, he wrestled with overwhelming fear. The building where he and his wife took their daughter for lunch some five short months ago, where he was supposed to take his other daughter in just a couple short years, was under attack. Accompanying the sight was a loud obnoxious sound he couldn't even describe. Immediately, the alarm system started blaring and the emergency lights were blinking, but Mr. Bianchi couldn't peel his eyes away from his window just yet. He knew the building was being evacuated. However, the sight he took in caused him to pray all the more. The sky that was so clear and blue immediately changed to black from the smoke pouring out. He could barely see one patch of blue anymore. Then his eyes were focused on pieces of debris flying out the windows. He spotted a telephone flying through the air toward his building along with other office items.

"Dear God," he muttered. "Why?"

He finally composed himself and grabbed his cell phone, briefcase, and, at the last minute, the picture sitting on his desk. It was taken quite a few years ago in Central Park when the girls were younger.

As he reached the door to his office, he unlocked his cell phone and scanned his favorites until he found his wife's number. He watched his shaky hands press the buttons and pushed the phone to his ear as it tried dialing. The first two times did not go through. He entered the crowd at the stairwell and joined as they began their trek down. He shook the phone and screamed at it to connect. Then miraculously, he heard it ring.

"Lisa, can you hear me?" Mr. Bianchi almost screamed into the phone. "Are you there?"

"Anthony! Yes, I can hear you." Mrs. Bianchi was weeping. "Are you okay? We just crossed through the tunnel when it happened. They won't let me back! They've closed everything! Jessica! Ashley!" Mrs. Bianchi was crying too hard to go on.

"Yes, I'm okay. They're evacuating us right now. I'll try to get to the girls, although I know they're smart enough to do the right thing. I'm sure the schools are keeping the kids until they feel it's safe to let them go. Just get to my parents' house, tell them I'm safe, and all of you start praying."

"Okay, I'll tell them. And Anthony…" She paused. "We haven't stopped."

CHAPTER 16

"But there were two loud crashes," Jessica whispered half to herself and half to anyone who would listen.

"What?" Ben whispered back.

"If that's really what we heard while we were in our classrooms, then where did the second crash come from?" All of a sudden, Jessica and Ben looked at each other and both gasped as they realized at the same exact moment what that meant.

"Another crash!" Jessica whispered, terrified, but not loudly enough to scare the others around her.

"Then that means, that both…" Ben let his words hang in the air as the two of them stared at each other in disbelief. They turned back to listen to Mr. Montanez as he continued.

"Two airplanes have attacked both of the Twin Towers. They believe it might be an act of terrorism. There is not much more to share with you at this point."

Jessica craned her neck toward the small staff room. Since the teachers were all in the community room attempting to comfort students, she was able to clearly watch the recording, confirming what Mr. Montanez just shared. She held her breath as a second airplane made its way into the picture and, just as they predicted, collided with the second tower. As much as Jessica wanted to look away, she couldn't. The horror of watching an airplane purposefully crash into a building, killing all the passengers, was more than Jessica could bear. But she couldn't look away. Half the airplane broke apart then, flying through the air until it finally landed blocks away.

One particular conversation replayed itself in Jessica's mind. The discussion she overheard among her parents at the start of summer vacation. *We had warning beforehand and we ignored it. This should have been prevented. What was happening to our country?* Jessica allowed these thoughts to engulf her mind for a minute.

Every student in the room was speechless. The teachers had composed themselves long enough to try to help the students. From the weight of the silence in the room, it seemed like a ton of bricks was hanging over everyone. Then slowly, a little at a time, students and adults began to sob together. First the younger ones, then slowly it spread across the entire room. Slowly, Jessica felt suffocated by a fear she had never felt before as the realization hit her like a cold bucket of water. Her father! Her dad! All her anger and resentment took a backseat as new emotions swept over her. *Was he inside the restaurant eating breakfast? Where was he? New Jersey?* Then another series of thoughts struck her. Her parents were supposed to bring her grandparents to New Jersey to visit her other grandparents today. She remembered a brief conversation between her parents just this morning about some phone call her father had to make at the last minute. She remembered the anger that rose deep in her soul as she wanted to scream at him as she questioned why his family wasn't enough for him anymore. Jessica began to panic as all these thoughts jumbled together in her mind. She mumbled something Ben couldn't understand.

"Haveta…haveta…home…Mom…Ash…my fa…" She couldn't seem to get her thoughts straight. "God, why?" she whispered. She stood up and through dazed eyes looked around the room. Was her father out there? She looked at the teachers who were standing along the walls with tear-streaked faces, unsure of how to help their students when they themselves were in shock. How many people with loved ones or friends in those buildings? Her eyes then moved down to her younger peers. The uncertainty of what just happened, but terror in their eyes. She looked around at her classmates and watched as diversity melted away, and students who had nothing in common put their arms around classmates to offer comfort. It seemed like hours when she had only been standing for a matter of seconds. Ben stood up next to her, but Jessica didn't notice.

Faltering as she tried to move, she knew she needed to get to the nearest exit to escape from the suffocating newscasters. But when she stumbled a couple steps, the room began to spin. She tripped and felt Ben's arms catch her around her shoulders as he eased her back down. Initially she resisted and attempted to push him away, but he only held on tighter. The tears couldn't be contained any longer, and Jessica wept onto his shoulder uncontrollably. She knew she had to get home to her mother and make sure her father was safe, but she couldn't seem to move.

Muffled voices caused her to look up, and she did as Mr. Montanez approached the microphone again. Through choked words, he asked the teachers to meet him in the front of the room. Jessica wanted to hear what they were saying, so she tried to pull herself together to stand up and get across the room. However, by the time she stood up, Mr. Montanez was back at the microphone.

"Boys and girls, this terrible event has us all feeling very vulnerable right now." He had to pause to get his tears under control before he continued, "But I'm going to ask you to find your homeroom teacher and gather together. We are going to remain down here for a while longer until we know it's safe to leave the building. Your teachers will be available to talk with you, cry with you, and offer support and answer questions to the best of their knowledge during our time together."

Jessica knew exactly where Mrs. West was. She felt relieved to have her as a homeroom teacher as well. Other than her parents and her youth pastor, Pastor Dan, and his wife, Mrs. Sherman, Mrs. West was the only other adult Jessica wanted to be with.

Ben stayed next to her as they wove their way through the sea of students and teachers to get to Mrs. West. Jessica felt like she had to cross the entire United States to get to her, but once she did, she collapsed and began sobbing again. Mrs. West wrapped her arms around everyone—girls and boys—together and cried along with them. Opening her eyes, Jessica caught a glimpse of Tom with his red swollen eyes.

Funny, she thought, *how in the face of adversity people are seen for who they truly are.* Not one critical or judgmental thought came into her head as she thought about him, but instead, she felt sorry for him.

"My mother's cousin works in Tower 1," one classmate said, turning Jessica's attention back to the group. "I only see her once a year at Christmas, but she has three children, all under the age of ten."

"My uncle is a security guard in the lobby of Tower 2," another girl replied. For a brief instant, Jessica wondered if she had ever seen the girl's uncle all those times she visited.

"I know lots of people who live in my apartment building who work in one of the towers."

"My aunt's father..."

"Our old neighbor..."

Mrs. West even shared that her husband left early in the morning for a business trip to San Francisco. She explained even though she hoped his flight would have already been beyond this area, fear tried to creep its way into her heart.

This last comment gave Jessica guilt feelings mixed with the fear she was already feeling. She had been wondering if they would ever stop, but then to hear Mrs. West express her fears gave new meaning to guilt for Jessica. She was old enough to know people dealt with tragedy differently, but she didn't feel like listening to these stories. Right now, she just wanted to know her dad was okay, but she knew she should feel empathy for her peers.

Her fear began to change and was replaced with an urgency to go home. "Mrs. West, when can we go home?"

"I'm not sure, honey. They want to make sure you are all kept as safe as possible, especially if we are being attacked."

"Attacked!" Jessica still couldn't believe those words. Who would want to attack the United States? She knew from her history classes that wars had always been present, dating back to biblical times. God gave His people strength to fight and win against many of their enemies, and He also allowed His people to be defeated when they turned their backs on Him. She was no stranger to all the Bible stories her mother had read to her through the years. But this is 2001. The world is more civilized now. We have a United Nations. The United States has one of the strongest military forces, or so she thought.

"Look." Ben was pointing to the doorway. Jessica followed his point. "What's going on over there?"

A sudden realization hit Jessica and hope began to fill her. "Those are parents! How did they get in?" The school door is always locked, and anyone who enters during school hours is buzzed in.

"Maybe we can go home now!" Tom's voice was filled with hope.

The class followed every move as Mr. Montanez came once again to the microphone. This time, his voice was under control, although the look still remained in his eyes. "Today, school will be closing early. Many of your parents have notified us that they will be coming to pick you up. Please remain where you are, and when you see them, you may get your things and leave. If your parents have not come, please remain where you are.

Do not leave the building without an adult. We will be calling those parents we have not heard from."

Scanning the crowd, Jessica searched for her mother but to no avail. She wasn't surprised. If they left according to schedule, they'd already be through the Holland Tunnel in New Jersey. Even if her mother was on her way, it would take her a long time to get there. Jessica's mind rested on her sister. Where is she? She must be terrified. Jessica desperately wished she had her cell phone with her so she could call her mother, but ever since her birthday, she had a terrible time remembering to charge it, so she left it home today sitting on the charger.

Jessica prayed that her mother would be there soon. Never being one to wait, Jessica liked to take matters into her own hands even if it meant reaping the consequences later. Even though her mother was constantly reminding her to wait on the Lord, for His timing is perfect. This was a tough lesson for her to learn but one that she would have a lot of opportunity to work on in the hours and days ahead.

"Ben, I need your help." Jessica grabbed his shirtsleeve and whispered in his ear, "I need you to distract Mrs. West. Get her to look the other way, away from the door. I need to go home *now*. Please, Ben!"

The look in Jessica's eyes was one of desperation. Ben struggled with strange feelings he didn't understand when he was around her, but he needed to keep a level head on his shoulders. "No way! You can't leave now," he whispered back. Then he looked around to see if anyone was paying attention to their conversation. He felt like they were screaming. But nobody seemed to pay them any mind. He figured they all had issues of their own right now. "Jessica, I know you're worried about your dad, but look around you. There's chaos everywhere! You don't know what's outside. Even if I let you go, you'll never get through the doors without an adult. I want to help you, but I can't let you do this. Listen, we live just down the street. I'm sure my mother will be here soon. Just wait with me and you can come to my place."

Jessica knew he'd say something like that. Ben had such a strong faith, even at the young age of fourteen, and she'd never known him to do anything against the rules. "Please!" she whispered as loud as she dared to. "I HAVE to get to my father. You have no idea what I'm feeling right now. Your father is safe and not anywhere near the towers." As soon as the words came out, Jessica regretted saying them. Ben's father was the owner of a chain of restaurants, and he often traveled all over the world helping others start their businesses. Right now, Ben's father was in Seattle, Washington, far away from the attacks. The look in Ben's eyes faltered but just for a moment before he spoke again.

"Even though my father *may* be safe, and we don't know if they've hit anywhere else, but even if he is, I can still understand what you're feeling, and I'm not going to let you do it. Besides, I'm sure he managed to get outside and away from the area as soon as he heard the first crash." Ben began praying that what he said was true. He believed God would help Jessica understand the danger of what she wanted to do and would give him wisdom in how to help her.

"Well then, you're just going to have to stop me, or join me." With that, Jessica scanned the room and began slowly scooting herself away from the class as Mrs. West was looking in the opposite direction. Jessica heard bits of what she was saying.

"My husband doesn't work in the Twin Towers but often meets clients there to discuss business. Thank God he's out of town on business and not coming home until tomorrow."

Jessica felt a pang of guilt. All she could think about was herself, and she didn't care about all the other students with family members that may have been affected. She completely forgot that Mr. West often went to the World Trade Center for business. Mrs. West was recently married, and while Jessica was worried about her father, she couldn't imagine being newly married and losing a spouse.

What was she doing? Ben shook his head in disbelief as he watched Jessica slowly and carefully slide her way through the people, creeping closer and closer to the door. He was torn between going with her and staying here where he should be. What if his mother came and he wasn't here? Ben was an only child, and his mother sometimes hovered over him a little too much, in his mind. He prayed quickly, knowing he only had a few seconds to act before Jessica was gone. Desperately, he turned to his buddy who was sitting near him. "Psst, Matt! Come here."

When Matt made himself so that he was right next to Ben, Ben continued, "I need your help, man. Please. I have to do something right now—something that I wouldn't normally do. Please don't ask me questions, just do it. You know me. I wouldn't ask you if it wasn't extremely important." As he saw the questions in Matt's eyes, he quickly continued so Matt wouldn't have time to ask, "If you're here when my mom comes, please get to her and let her know I'm not here but I'm safe and will be home before tonight."

Immediately, he turned and began following Jessica, scooting his way along. He briefly replayed the look in Matt's eyes as he left, praying once more that Matt wouldn't tell on him. If he knew his friend, and he thought he did, Matt would do exactly as Ben asked him, even if it meant staying at the school after his mother arrived to wait for Ben's mom.

CHAPTER 17

It was slow moving, down all those flights of stairs, but Mr. Bianchi finally stepped outside. What he saw made him want to turn around and go back in. The sky that was so blue and clear minutes ago was now covered with a thick gray cloud that seemed endless. The amount of smoke billowing out of the North Tower caused him to consider how anyone could survive in there breathing it in.

Chaos was everywhere. People were running all around the streets seemingly without any real purpose. The crew from "Ten House," or the fire station next to his building, had already entered the North Tower. Sirens were blaring in the distance, and Mr. Bianchi saw flashing lights racing their way down toward him. Then, he heard another airplane. *Oh, good*, he thought. *It's about time someone came to rescue the victims.* But just then, he looked up and understanding hit him like a thunder bolt. This second airplane was heading toward the South Tower, right in front of him!

The sound was deafening, forcing Mr. Bianchi to cover his ears. He stood there and just watched as the second plane struck the South Tower with a blasting sound. He didn't have to look around him to know he was not alone. Standing like statues, mouths agape, people watched the scene unfolding before them.

This is the beginning of the end, he thought. He began to pray for guidance. Even though his family was in his mind, he knew they were safe at their schools. He felt a strong pull to make his way across Liberty Street and over to the towers to see how he could help. As he began, he willed himself to keep his eyes focused on what was in front of him and not what was falling out of the towers above him.

With determination, he fought against a crowd of people unsure of where to go. As he approached the South Tower, he began searching for someone in command. It didn't take long to find a fire chief surrounded by a few dozen rescue workers. Mr. Bianchi walked right up to him without a second thought.

"Where do you want me?"

"What?" Mr. Bianchi could see he caught the chief off guard but only briefly. He watched as the man sized him up and down, and it was only then he realized he had left his briefcase with the picture somewhere on the sidewalk across the street. All he had was his cell phone in its case attached to his belt loop. "Are you sure you want to do this?"

"Yes, I need to help. Stop wasting time and tell me where I can be of the most help to you." Mr. Bianchi realized his voice may have been a bit harsher than he intended, but he didn't like wasting time when he could be saving people.

"Fine. Fanning, Rimms, take this man with your group." The chief looked back to Mr. Bianchi. "They're going into the lobby to set up a command post and to disperse their men around the building. Good luck. You're gonna need it. And if you believe in a god, I'd start praying." He shook his head as he made this last comment, turning back to the remaining few who would stay with him until they were needed.

CHAPTER 18

Jessica glanced behind her and saw Ben scooting along after her. She felt the butterflies again in her stomach as realization hit her. Ben was coming with her. While she would have done this by herself, she had to admit she was glad for the company. Knowing it was Ben somehow gave her a sense of peace she hadn't felt since she heard the news.

She turned back and continued moving slowly toward her target, joining in random conversations here and there with classes as she moved. The teachers didn't care at this point. Older students were searching for their younger siblings to comfort them, and even the teachers were wandering a few steps to talk amongst their colleagues.

Getting to the door wasn't as difficult as Jessica thought it would be. Now it was a matter of getting past the administrators and parents crowded in the doorways. But she needn't have worried, for just as she heard Ben creep up behind her, Ms. King walked to the other set of doors to comfort a frantic mother. Jessica looked around for Mr. Montanez, but she remembered someone had to be up in the office to let the parents in. Assuming it would be him, she took her chance.

Targeting a group of mothers huddled together just inside the doorway, Jessica stood and slowly, so as not to call attention to herself, walked over toward the group. Briefly she caught Emily's eye on the other side of the room and waved before leaving the room with the group and Ben by her side.

Making it this far, Jessica began to wonder how they would get past the office since she was sure that was the only door open to parents. As they reached the top of the first flight of stairs, Ben grabbed her elbow and led her through a doorway down a small hallway toward a set of doors with a big exit sign overhead. She wanted to ask him how he knew about this way but thought it best not to say anything until they were a safe distance from the school.

As Ben pushed her through the doorway, Jessica was ready to shield her eyes from the sun. Once outside, however, what she saw was far worse than a blinding sun. Grey smoke that was like one hundred times the typical New York City smog poured across the sky. Sirens were blaring everywhere, and as Jessica looked around, women were screaming, men were running, and officials from NYFD and NYPD were shouting out orders. Jessica thought about turning back, away from the horror of it all, but knew she had to get to her parents.

"Are you sure you want to do this?" She had completely forgotten Ben was standing right behind her. "It's like we're trapped in a nightmare about to wake up."

Jessica couldn't even talk, so she just nodded. As they began making their way down Hudson Street toward Cornerstone, inching closer to the World Trade

Center, she lost her balance as people ran past her pushing and shoving to get to their loved ones. One man, with the NYPD, stopped and questioned why they were by themselves and not with an adult. Jessica, who was never at a loss for words, opened her mouth to answer, but all that came out was a choking sound. Ben answered for them both.

"We were with our mother, officer, but we turned away for just a minute, and when we turned back, she was ahead of us. She is just up that way a bit." Even as he said the words, Ben felt guilt and regret rise up inside him. *Please forgive me, Lord. I'm sorry.* He was not one to lie and hated the way it made him feel inside. Silently, he made himself a reminder to make it up to God.

"Okay, but you'd better hurry and catch up to her. This is no place for two kids to be alone right now." The officer turned back to concentrate on directing traffic.

Jessica looked at Ben with grateful eyes. She didn't need to say anything. Her eyes said it all. He nodded and smiled, understanding her look.

They continued to walk on in silence, taking in the panic that was engulfing them on all sides. Neither one of them had ever seen the city like this. Jessica turned and felt consumed by screams and terror in every direction. Her gaze would alternate between the people around them and the smoke billowing from the towers.

Ben saw the frightened look in her eyes, so he took her hand as he led the way through a group of onlookers standing outside an apartment building. They reached Cornerstone School. In a matter of minutes, Jessica found Ashley and was given permission to take her as the staff knew her. She then led her to the tiny grassy area close to the school, off the sidewalk. They stood hugging while Ashley sobbed into Jessica's arms. Ben knew Jessica was just as scared, and he struggled with hugging them both or leaving them be. He finally decided on letting them have this moment as he heard Jessica utter a prayer for their parents, their safety, and finally—peace.

Ben was the first to speak after the prayer ended. "What is going on here? The whole world's gone crazy. It's like the battle of Armageddon."

Jessica closed her eyes to relieve herself of what she was looking at. She had read bits and pieces of the book of Revelation, and, of course, her mother had discussed with the girls when a world event occurred. However, she didn't know as much as Ben, and that fact bothered her. She wished she had listened more when her mother suggested she read her Bible every day. Then maybe she wouldn't have such a knot in her stomach.

Sensing the panic that threatened to consume her, Ben knew he needed to be strong for her. Recovering himself, he spoke quietly the words his father always recited to him during difficult times.

"Those who wait on the Lord shall renew their strength. We will mount up with wings like eagles."

Jessica's eyes sprung open like a tightly wound coil. Turning to him, she asked, "What did you just say?"

Ben just looked at her and continued the passage from the prophet Isaiah, "We will run and not grow weary. We will walk and not faint."

Not believing her ears, Jessica once again found comfort in these words. As she looked to the sky, she closed her eyes and imagined herself as an eagle soaring above the storm, relying solely on God's wind.

"Now, I don't know what's going on, but I do know that I need you to calm down if we are going to continue to try to find your father." The determination in Ben's voice mixed with emotion was new to Jessica's ears, but it also brought her comfort.

Jessica took a deep breath, speaking as she exhaled, "Okay, I'm calm. Let's keep moving."

It was only then that Ashley spoke, "Wait a minute. Aren't we going home to wait for Mom and Dad?"

Jessica knew this was going to be difficult for her sister. However, Ashley didn't understand what she was feeling. This morning had been one of those days where she had smart-mouthed her father and had left without apologizing. Now she was desperate to make it right. "Ash, if you want to go home, we can take you there. But I can't until I at least try to find Dad. He's still down there. I know he is. If he's alive, he'd be the first one to help. You know that. We've got to get to him." Ashley only nodded as she fought back the tears. She did know that, but hoped Ben would be able to talk some sense into her sister.

Ben reached for Jessica's hand. Had it been any other day, she would have dwelt on the butterflies. But right now, though she felt a brief moment of excitement, Jessica's main focus was on finding her father. They made their way easily enough for a bit longer, but once they hit West Broadway it was like a body traffic jam. Everyone seemed to be either running away from the catastrophe, or running toward it, determined to find a loved one. Some people just stood there as if they seemed lost. Jessica tightened her grip on Ben and her sister, all of a sudden very much aware of her own mortality.

After traveling only one block down West Broadway, the trio was approaching Chambers Street when Jessica was bumped by a NYC police officer running past them. She heard something on his radio about the Pentagon.

"Ben," she cried out to him, "did you hear that?"

"Hear what exactly?" Ben had a point. There was so much noise around them. "What was I supposed to hear?"

"Something on that officer's radio. It was about the Pentagon."

Other people must have somehow found out also because, all of a sudden, conversations revolved around the Pentagon and American Airlines Flight 77. Jessica felt her legs turn to rubber.

CHAPTER 19

A nightmare. That's what this was. Mr. Bianchi attempted to reassure himself with this possibility as he made his way into the South Tower with the group. He looked around him at their jackets. Already there were a number of different stations represented here. He felt heaviness in his heart as he pushed his way through the doors and looked up at the flags still hanging from the balcony. His thoughts switched to his dear Jessica and how much she loved looking at them. As he choked back a sob, he mumbled a quick prayer. One of his favorite verses came to mind, and he began repeating it to himself. "For I know the thoughts that I think toward you. Thoughts of peace and not of evil."

He could think about his family later. They were safe, he felt it. Now he needed to devote his complete attention to his present situation. He looked around at the mass of people exiting the building. Even though the South Tower wasn't officially evacuated until it was hit, there were already hundreds of people escorted through the doors out to Liberty Street as far away from the Center as possible.

Focusing his attention back on the job at hand, Fanning and Rimms had already set up an operating post identical to the one in the North Tower lobby. They assigned their men to various jobs. Mr. Bianchi watched as everyone from NYPD, NYFD, and Port Authority seemed to know exactly what to do. Praying for guidance, Mr. Bianchi headed to the closest stairwell ready to fight against the crowd of evacuees until someone needed his help.

It didn't take long before he knew where he was needed. He had just approached the landing to the fifth floor when he heard crying above him. Looking up, he saw a woman, probably in her mid-sixties, clinging to the railing. Her face was covered in blood, and her dress was torn. She had one shoe on her foot with a heel at least two inches high. He noticed her hair, once pulled back in a tight bun, was now pulled apart, sticking to the blood on her face. She seemed too frozen to move.

Mr. Bianchi slowly made his way through the throngs of people still coming down the stairwell. When he finally reached her, he eased her fingers off the railing and gently lifted her shaking body into his arms as he reassured her she was going to be okay. She gripped her fingers together around his neck as he turned to begin the slow trek back down the stairs. He asked her name and found out she was the wife of a CEO from one of the companies upstairs.

"I work as an office assistant on the seventh floor, and when Tower 1 was hit, I knew something was terribly wrong. I immediately tried to get upstairs to my husband. The elevators were jammed, so I knew I could make it up the stairs more quickly. As I worked my way up, I was trampled and dragged along back down by people trying to leave. Even though Port Authority urged everyone in Tower 2 to remain in their offices so those in the North Tower could evacuate easier, there were still hundreds of people in the South Tower who didn't listen and evacuated anyways. I couldn't get myself right before I was trampled again. Finally, I managed to get myself over to the side and grabbed the railing, fearing for my life."

Listening patiently, Mr. Bianchi tried to appear calm but clenched his teeth as she concluded her story and did all he could not to reveal his anger. He couldn't believe this! How many people had come out of this building and yet not one could take a moment and help this poor woman? *What had this world come to*, he wondered.

"Well, ma'am, you're safe now. Do you think you can walk the rest of the way? We only have a couple more flights to go."

"Yes, I think I'm all right," Mrs. Soan replied. However, as Mr. Bianchi lowered her to the landing on the fourth floor, she crumbled to the floor. Mr. Bianchi reached for her, and it was only then that he noticed how swollen her ankle was. There was no doubt in his mind it was broken. He lifted her once again, and they continued the walk with the rest of the group down, each step one closer to freedom.

CHAPTER 20

They somehow made it to Warren Street, and Jessica was quite relieved when Ben pulled her hand, indicating for her to follow him across West Broadway, down her familiar street. She instinctively looked around in search of her parents, knowing they wouldn't be there but hoping just the same. All she saw, however, was more of the same. The sirens were much louder now, and NYC fire trucks from all around Manhattan were still flying by, trying desperately to get down to the World Trade Center.

"God," she silently prayed, "what is going on here? Are You trying to get our attention? If so, I think you've got it. Is this a punishment? Please forgive us if so. I'm so sorry. Please keep my parents safe and help me find my dad. And please forgive me for leaving school the way I did." Then she added, "And thank You so much for bringing Ben here with us. I think I would have been lost without him."

Something happened inside Jessica that normally didn't happen. She felt a fluttering. A "quickening of her spirit" as her mother often called it. It was almost as if she heard a quiet whisper amidst the sounds around her that said, "*For I know the thoughts that I think toward you. Thoughts of peace and not of evil.* Jessica couldn't believe it! For the second time since she heard the news, she felt almost a peace that couldn't be explained. She knew the Lord would be there to help them.

"Did you hear me?" Jessica heard a hint of annoyance in Ben's voice.

"I'm sorry, what did you say?" Even though she knew Ben would understand what had just happened, she preferred not to say anything just yet.

"I said the Pentagon was hit by another plane. I heard some people talking about how it's the latest all over the TV."

So, she had heard correctly. For the first time, Jessica took a good long look around her. Most people were crying, while some of them were just staring down to where the two towers fumed with smoke. Many of them were on their cell phones trying to connect with loved ones.

As they reached her building, (Jessica would always thank God for years to come that she somehow ended up right near her home), the threesome decided someone should go inside to make sure nobody was home before moving on to find their father. Ashley readily volunteered. She quickly pushed through the doors and headed for the familiar elevator.

Waiting outside, Jessica and Ben discussed the quickest route down. They agreed to follow Church Street all the way to Liberty Street as long as the roads were still open. Jessica looked around and found most of the people passing them now were spectators, although they saw many EMS paramedics or rescue workers rushing down Church Street to help.

While lost in her thoughts, standing there with Ben on the sidewalk and waiting for Ashley, the entire city seemed to freeze. A loud noise filled the air unlike anything they had ever heard before. It seemed slightly familiar to Jessica. Then it hit her. One night, she watched a documentary with her father about skyscrapers destroyed in an earthquake. She couldn't remember what country it happened in, but the noise was the same nonetheless. Nobody moved as everyone's eyes focused on the towers. The South Tower began to creak and rumble. Jessica felt like she was stuck in a horror movie with what happened next. The South Tower began to violently shake, and the noise they heard was bending steel. Small objects seemed to be falling out the windows of both buildings, racing down to the ground. Only after a few blinks did Jessica realize they were people.

"Oh my gosh," she managed to breathe out.

CHAPTER 21

One more flight. That's all Mr. Bianchi had left when he heard it. They all heard it—every single person in the stairwell heard it. He had no doubt what was about to happen since he had watched enough documentaries to know exactly what he was hearing. It was bending steel. At first, he thought it might have been from the North Tower since it had been hit first. However, it didn't take him long to know that was just wishful thinking. The sound was definitely surrounding him. He felt like he was in the center of a steel prison, and he knew if they didn't get out soon they would be under 1,500,000 tons of metal. Even worse, he knew out of the hundreds of people above him remaining, many would not see another blue sky on this earth. Quickening his pace a bit, Mr. Bianchi considered himself fit, yet he was having trouble catching his breath with the extra weight of Mrs. Soan. He silently chided himself for letting too many things get in his way of his health, and he told himself he would listen to his wife and get back in shape if he made it out of there.

Finally, they reached the lobby. As he struggled through the doorway, they heard another sound—more fierce than before. Mr. Bianchi knew it was a matter of time before there would be no chance of survival. Getting a second wind, he bolted into the street. Bumped from behind, the twosome stumbled to the ground. Mrs. Soan rolled out of his arms. The last thing Mr. Bianchi remembered was watching that nice lady drag herself onto the curb, directly in front of his building, then swept up by an EMS worker.

CHAPTER 22

World Trade Center, Tower 2, South Tower, no longer existed. Disappearing from view, it collapsed into a giant heap of rubble. Smoke and debris appeared everywhere. Jessica couldn't move. Around her, people were shocked back into reality, wailing out loved ones' names, running into doorways for protection, and some fainting from the shock.

Jessica's head begin to spin. Different thoughts flooded into her mind like one of those video clips where they shoot a bunch of different scenes, and by the time you blink, they're on to the next one already. As she stared at the big hole filling with what looked to her like smoke, she saw images of when she was young, sitting atop her father's shoulders as they walked with her mother down to the Center for a Saturday lunch in the mall. The next image appeared just as instantly, but this time, she was around five, walking in between her parents while Ashley was seated on their father's shoulders. She and her mother were holding hands, singing a song she learned in kindergarten about numbers. The sky was overcast and just cloudy enough to feel like rain.

Immediately, the next image appeared, and this time, Jessica was standing in the lobby of the South

Tower admiring all the flags of the countries. At eight years old, she finally understood their meaning. She was learning about her heritage and family history in second grade. Identifying the corresponding flags was one of the lessons. At first, she tried to memorize them all but quickly realized that was impossible, so she just looked for the Italian, German, and French flags since they were the ones of her ancestors.

Once again, flash! Another image appeared. This one was not too long ago. She was inside the Warner Brothers Studio store where she and Ashley used to have fun trying on different hats and sunglasses. On this particular day, she was feeling too old to fool around like that, and she was waiting impatiently for her parents to finish talking with one of Mr. Bianchi's coworkers who they happened to bump into that day. Feeling anxious to get over to the Gap to buy a new sweatshirt she had seen, Jessica remembered rolling her eyes at her immature sister who had called to her while wearing a pair of Tweety Bird sunglasses.

The next image was a brief picture of New York City and the harbor the first time Jessica was taken to the observation deck of the South Tower. She felt her breath taken away again just like that first day as she looked around her in awe of the beauty of her home.

The last image was a montage of flashing pictures one after the other. It was too disturbing for Jessica, but she couldn't seem to remove it from her thoughts even as she shook her head trying. It was her birthday, the day her parents took her to the Windows on the World restaurant. She saw her father's building as she glued her eyes onto the door waiting for him to walk through, and then she saw him give her the big hug as he greeted her with his special nickname for her, "Peanut." She saw the elevator doors open and the doorway to the restaurant. She saw David, the young server who so graciously attended to their every need.

Like a flash, it was all gone. She felt herself being shaken, and somewhere far away, her name was said repeatedly.

"Jessica…Jessica! We've got to turn away."

She finally came back to reality and felt Ben's hands on her arms, shaking her slightly. Looking down at him, she realized his face was directly in front of hers.

"Are you okay? I thought I lost you there for a bit." She saw the concern in his eyes.

"Uh, I think so. No—yes, I…" Jessica realized all those images that appeared to her only took a handful of seconds even though it felt a lot longer. She had to glance over Ben's shoulder to check if what she thought she just saw really happened. Ben must have realized what she was doing and saw the change in her eyes.

"It's not a dream, Jessica. The South Tower just collapsed. We need to get you inside. It won't be long before we are covered."

Jessica didn't understand. Covered with what? But she didn't want to know right now. "I can't go home! I need to find my father!" Jessica struggled between hysteria and trying to focus her thoughts once more on the eagle soaring peacefully, trusting in God. Ben understood the urgency she felt and, as a result, managed to remain the calm and sensible one even though he would remember for months how shaken up he really was inside.

"I have to find my father!" Jessica realized she was shouting at him now. She struggled to control herself, but her body was shaking too violently. "Please, Ben, you don't understand," she cried, grabbing him by the shoulders. "If you understand like you say you do, then help me. I need to get to the bank." What if it was too late? What if her father was dead, and she never had the chance to tell him once more that she loved him? That she appreciated him? She couldn't remember the last time she told him she loved him.

Ben saw the look in her eyes and knew it showed only one thing—terror. Jessica was beyond fear. She was terrified. He thought he understood. The world they both knew was falling to pieces around them. The fear inside him mixed with strange feelings he felt toward her. Feelings that told him he didn't want to bring her home just so he could stay near her longer. He realized he enjoyed being with her and looked forward to seeing her. These were new feelings, but he realized another feeling he held. A longing to protect her. No. A *need* to protect her. *He* wanted to be the one to keep her safe from harm. *He* wanted to be the one to help her find her father. *He* wanted her to come to him seeking comfort. These feelings bothered him a little, yet he didn't want them to disappear.

Bringing his thoughts captive, Ben wanted to do what was right. So he silently began praying for wisdom. *God, I want to help her. I see the look in her eyes. But I want to keep her safe. Please tell me what to do. Show me so I can do what is right by You.*

As he opened his eyes, Jessica was looking at him. For a brief instant, she relaxed her body and knew. He was praying, and now his eyes showed peace, something she had been struggling with through the morning. How easily it seemed for that verse that occupied her thoughts to be swept away by the terror around her.

She leaned against him as he put his arms around her. The tears came then for both of them. They wept together for their home. They wept for all those innocent people trapped inside the World Trade Center. They wept for the people who had died on those airplanes and inside the building.

After they wept and felt like they could weep no more, Ben held on to her and began to pray. Jessica closed her eyes as she listened and let herself relax against his body.

Just as he finished praying, he was about to give in to her desire to look for her father when Ashley came out with a defeated look on her tear-stained face. She ran into her sister's open arms as her whole body shook. Jessica knew what it meant. Nobody was home.

Ben wrapped the sisters in his arms and all three released their emotions for what just occurred. As they composed themselves as best they could, they took a step to help Jessica fulfill her only mission. Stopping short in their steps, they didn't get far before they heard another sound just as terrifying as one they heard about a half hour ago. They all looked back to where now only the single North Tower stood. The trio stood, staring once more, as the North Tower began to tremble and collapse. It looked to Jessica as if it was all happening in slow motion. She felt her legs shake and feared she would collapse onto the sidewalk just like the way the towers had.

"Ben…" she whispered.

She grabbed his arm and clung to it with both hands to steady herself. In return, he put one arm around her for support.

"I know," he acknowledged. He had never seen anything so disastrous in his life. His grandfather had told him plenty of stories about family members who had been persecuted during the Holocaust. The Millers were Jewish and had left their home in Germany shortly before the Second World War to come to the United States. They changed their name from Miler, the Jewish spelling, to Miller, a more common Americanized spelling. They found a church that believed in the death and resurrection of Jesus Christ, their Messiah. But Mr. Miller never forgot his heritage and what his family went through. Raising his son, Ben, a Christian, Mr. Miller also took pride in knowing they were God's chosen people. He made sure he did everything he could to instill this knowledge in his son.

So while Jessica had learned about what happened to the Jewish people in history class, Ben felt like he lived it. He had pictures of relatives who lived through the concentration camps and were torn in the middle of the night from the only home they ever knew.

Now, he was the one living through the terror. Here he was, similar to those family members, watching the only life he ever knew fall apart right in front of his eyes, yet completely helpless to do anything about it.

Looking down at Jessica, Ben felt sympathy for her. She was so naïve. Things like this didn't happen today in this country. This was something to read about in history books or to hear about on the news. How were they going to get through this? What had he gotten himself into?

"God." Ben almost breathed the word. God was how they were going to get through.

Jessica began coughing, bringing Ben back to reality. They looked down the street and saw what looked like thick smoke, only it was pulverized concrete from the collapse. It made its way steadily across the city, block by block, engulfing everything in its way like a massive swarm of bees heading back to the hive.

"C'mon, I will not take no for an answer this time. We've got to get inside."

Forcing herself to nod, Jessica allowed herself to be turned from the horror around her and led back toward her building. Just then, something came over her, and there was nowhere else she wanted to be except in the comfort of her own home, away from the destruction playing out before her eyes in the only world she'd ever known.

CHAPTER 23

Safe within the walls of their apartment, the girls settled on the couch in front of the TV while Ben went for the landline to try to call his mother. She picked up on the first ring. "Mom! Yes, I'm safe. I'm at the Bianchi's apartment on Warren Street. Yes, we saw it all. I know, I'm sorry."

Jessica could only assume Ben's mother was beside herself with worry about him. No doubt she had seen Matt at school. Just then, her attention was brought back to the television screen. The announcer was talking about Flight 93 that had been headed for San Francisco. Jessica didn't hear anymore. She recalled what Mrs. West told the class that morning. Jessica hoped her husband wasn't on that plane, but an uneasy feeling swept over her.

Mayor Giuliani appeared and interrupted the replays. All three children stood unmoving, waiting to hear what the mayor had to say.

"Mom, just a minute. Turn on your TV if it's not already on." Ben didn't want to miss whatever was about to be said at this press conference.

The mayor talked about what happened and everyone's safety. Then he said words that filled Jessica with dread. "Evacuation of Lower Manhattan."

"What does that mean, Jess?" Ashley interrupted the press conference causing Jessica to miss what else was being said. "Do we have to leave New York?"

Poor Ashley, Jessica thought. She looked so young and weak today, even though she could take on Jessica to an arm wrestle challenge any typical day of the week. Jessica then wondered what she must look like, but quickly dismissed it from her mind.

"The mayor just issued an evacuation of Lower Manhattan. That means we need to leave here immediately."

"Not yet. I'll be right back." Ashley jumped off the couch and hurried to her room, only to return seconds later with Snowball, the stuffed kitten she slept with every night.

"Mom, did you catch that? We have to evacuate… I'm not sure where to go. Wait for us. We'll be there as soon as we can."

With Ben's father away on business, Ben knew he needed to step up and take responsibility for his mother and himself. He looked to Jessica with a question in his eyes. "Any idea where to go? Everything I know is here."

What would her parents do? Where were they? Was her mother safe? How about her father? She wished she knew more. The sound of the telephone startled her. She jumped up to grab it. "Hello? Mom? Dad?"

"Jessica, oh, thank God, you're safe!"

"Mom! Where are you? Are you okay? Where's Dad?" Jessica couldn't keep the tears from flowing onto her cheeks. "I'm so scared. Mayor Giuliani just issued an evacuation. Where do we go? Ashley and Ben and I are here. What if Daddy can't get out?" The questions from the past two hours brought themselves to the surface, comforting Jessica while talking to her mother.

"Ashley's with you? Oh, I'm so glad. I called your schools and they told me you girls had left already, but nobody could tell me who came to get you. I talked to your father earlier. He was about to evacuate his building. I have tried him since, but I can't get through. Your grandparents and I were on our way to New Jersey when the first crash hit. The Holland Tunnel is closed right now, but we are safe at Nana and Nonno's house. I wanted to drop your grandparents off before finding a way to come get you girls. In the meantime, there's only one place I want you to be. Get to the church as quickly as you can. I'll meet you there. I'm not going to rest until I have you two with me. But, honey, until then, remember Psalm 91."

Jessica could have kicked herself. Of course, her mother wanted them to get to their church. She had no doubt Pastor Gary and Pastor Dan would be there with their families as well as many others. She was sure of it!

"Okay, Mom, but hurry."

Before Mrs. Bianchi could urge Jessica to take care of herself and Ashley, the line cut out. She dialed the number again but heard a busy signal. She then tried Jessica's cell phone, but that also went right to her voicemail. "Oh, God, take care of my babies," she cried.

CHAPTER 24

Ben and Ashley both agreed with Jessica's mother, so after the girls quickly grabbed a few things and stuffed them into their backpacks, the trio headed out again. She wasn't sure it would help, but Jessica grabbed a few scarves to cover their mouths with. This time, their plan was to move in the opposite direction as swiftly as they could.

Jessica thought about how many people in history have had to evacuate their homes and how many have actually returned. Her mind focused specifically on the Jews, God's chosen people. She also thought about her father's family, leaving their home in Italy to come here to make a new life for themselves.

She was afraid. Afraid of the what-ifs. What if their building collapsed? What if something happened and the entire city was annihilated? But most importantly, what if her father was on his way home right now and didn't know where they went?

Of course, he would know. The one place her family considered their home away from home is Lower Manhattan Christian Church. This was the place where Jessica and Ashley spent every Sunday since they could remember, where Jessica spent her Wednesday nights with the youth group, and where she met Sami.

Just thinking about going there gave Jessica a feeling of peace—a peace that passes all understanding. She reflected on the verses her mother had uttered a few moments ago, Psalm 91, one of Mrs. Bianchi's favorite chapters in the Bible, which had also become one of her favorites, that talked about staying safe. Jessica recalled the first verse, "He who dwells in the secret place of the Most High shall abide under the shadow of the Almighty." She closed her eyes as she attempted to put herself under God's shadow like under a beautiful tree on a hot day. She somehow knew everything would be all right, even though they seemed to be walking through the valley of the shadow of death.

As they walked back outside, the dust from the concrete smacked them hard. They covered their faces and began running. They slowed down on West Broadway, which gave Jessica the opportunity to look over to Ashley. She felt compassion for her sister, the confusion and fear showing on her face. Jessica didn't know what they would do once Ben met his mother. Would she want to go with them? She put her hand on her sister's arm and gave her a smile when Ashley looked over at her.

The dust subsided a bit as they made their way further north. Nobody said much for the majority of the walk. It was a time of processing what was happening while, at the same time, it took all the strength they had to maneuver the crowds. They didn't need to use extra energy by talking, which would only slow them down.

Surprisingly, they found their way to Ben's house rather quickly despite the multitudes of people pushing their way up the street. Mrs. Miller was outside already waiting for them. When she saw Ben, she ran to him and held on like a mother afraid of losing her only son. After brief introductions were made, Mrs. Miller shared that her husband was safe, still in Seattle due to the closing of JFK Airport. Ben explained their plan of which Mrs. Miller was in complete agreement with to Jessica's great relief. The foursome started off back toward Church Street, which they would follow all the way up to Greene Street. As they crossed over West Broadway, Jessica stopped to turn around. On a typical day like today, the view of the towers would be one worth drawing, the way they looked, living up to their name as they towered over the smaller buildings while the sun gleamed off the windows. Now all they saw as they looked was one large, dark cloud. Jessica choked back a sob as she turned away and took Ashley's hand. On the other side of her, Ben reached for her free hand, and together, the four of them headed north, away from the engulfing terror. Jessica didn't know what tomorrow would bring, but she knew then and there that she would find her father no matter what the cost.

CHAPTER 25

With trembling fingers, Mrs. Bianchi gratefully accepted the cup of hot tea her mother handed her. Feeling nothing, she numbly drank the liquid out of duty rather than she wanted it. Staring at the television set, she asked no one in particular, "How could I be so stupid to leave my babies all day? What was I thinking?"

"You're not stupid, dear." Her mother sat on the arm of the couch, gently stroking her daughter's hair. "You had no idea this was going to happen today. You did absolutely nothing wrong. Only God knew. And those awful—"

"God knew…yes, God knew!" Mrs. Bianchi seemed to come alive as she started to quote Psalm 91:9–10. "Because you have made the Lord, *who* is my refuge, *Even* the Most High, your dwelling place, No evil shall befall you, Nor shall any plague come near your dwelling." Before long, all five were praying for their loved ones' safety, trusting God to take care of them.

While they were praying, an update was announced, so their attention was once more turned back to the television. "Oh, Mom, I'm so scared." Mrs. Bianchi accepted the loving arms of her mother as they wrapped around her. "What if the girls can't get to the church? What if Anthony can't find them? I'm so glad you're here with me."

"Ssh, hush now, don't talk like that. Trust God always and fully. Remember Proverbs 3:5. He knows what He is doing."

CHAPTER 26

Lower Manhattan Christian Church was an old refurbished building that sat on the relatively quiet one-way cobblestone road called Greene Street. They had moved to a few different locations during Jessica's life, and so even though it was still called Lower Manhattan Christian Church its current location was above Canal Street. Jessica didn't really think about the coincidence until she overheard two women as they were crossing Canal Street. One woman was so relieved she had good friends in Upper Manhattan.

"Even if the mayor didn't evacuate us, I still would have packed a bag and left. At least for a few days. It's just not safe down here right now."

"You really think it's much safer a few blocks above Canal Street?" the other woman countered. "I'm heading home to my apartment to pack my bags. As soon as the airport reopens, I'm catching a flight to visit my family in New Mexico. There's nothing out there that would attract terrorists."

Realization suddenly dawned on Jessica. God's protection was once again on them. How amazing that Mayor Giuliani evacuated the area below Canal Street, and yet here she was, able to walk to her second home, LMCC!

Jessica then shivered at the thought of what might have happened if they didn't have a church to go to. Her father was missing, her mother was somewhere in New Jersey trying to get back to the city. She and Ashley would have been so lonely. All of a sudden, a feeling of complete hopelessness threatened to wash over Jessica but was quickly followed by complete awe and amazement. God was in control of everything. He cared enough about her and her sister to make sure they had a safe place to go to until they saw their parents again.

As they approached the church, they were met by a group of church members offering a safe place to anyone who came by. "Jessica, Ashley, thank God you're safe!" Pastor Dan always knew just what to say. Jessica felt a swell of tears rise up in her eyes. Pastor Dan's wife, Alyson Sherman, stepped over from behind him and embraced the two girls. No words were needed. They were home.

Jessica was standing in the buffet line set up by members of her church behind Ashley and in front of Sami. Sami's family arrived shortly prior to Jessica. Ben and his mother were on the other side of the room typically used as a sanctuary, talking with a woman who had introduced herself and her son. He was just a year older than Ben. Jessica felt so safe and peaceful here. This was her home right now. She felt that whatever happened in the next few days, weeks, or months, until she knew where her father was, she could handle it as long as she was surrounded by her family here.

After the girls filled their plates, Pastor Dan and Mrs. Sherman gathered together the large group of youth that had been pouring into the church with their families and took them to the back room where they usually met for youth meetings. Ben was among them. Jessica noticed how at home and comfortable he seemed even though this was not his church. She settled into a chair between Ashley and Sami, ready to hear what Pastor Dan had to say.

"The book of Joel offers great advice for a time like this. In a way, it is a comfort to me knowing that this book was written so many years ago yet is so appropriate for today. It's almost like God intended to write these particular verses just for us." Pastor Dan chuckled before continuing, "Well, since He is God, He did know they could help us. So let's use what He has given us and take these words as a comfort. Cover yourselves with them as you listen. The first chapter of Joel, verse fourteen, 'Consecrate a fast, call a sacred assembly; gather the elders and all the inhabitants of the land into the house of the Lord your God, and cry out to the Lord. Alas, for the day! For the day of the Lord is at hand; it shall come as destruction from the Almighty.'"

He flipped a page and continued, "Chapter 2, 'For the day of the Lord is coming, for it is at hand: a day of darkness and gloominess, a day of clouds and thick darkness... "Now, therefore," says the Lord, "Turn to Me with all your heart, with fasting, with weeping, and with mourning." So rend your heart, and not your garments; return to the Lord your God, for He is gracious and merciful, slow to anger, and of great kindness.'"

Jessica found herself first thinking about the day of clouds and thick darkness. Wasn't that exactly what today looked like? Then her thoughts began questioning the last part Pastor Dan read. How could a gracious and merciful God allow this to happen? Was it that simple? Did they just need to repent and return to God? Jessica then remembered what she thought about the two towers. They were built by man. They represented strength to our nation. And for the first time, she actually grasped the meaning of what her mother had taught her, about credit being given to God, not to man. Was man being so proud that this was a punishment? But what Pastor Dan read next brought back her thoughts.

"Joel 2:32, 'And it shall come to pass that whoever calls on the name of the Lord shall be saved.'" He was quiet for a while then, letting the group take it all in. Knowing there would be questions, he was taking the moment to pray for wisdom to give answers that might help these kids.

For the next hour, Pastor Dan and Mrs. Sherman fielded questions from the group. While Jessica had no answers as to why it all happened, she felt better knowing God would take care of them. Pastor Dan closed with a prayer, not only for the families in New York City, but around the country too. He then ended with John 16:33 before dismissing the group.

"Wow, what a powerful pep talk, don't you think?" Jessica spun around to find Ben behind her. "I mean, all those verses written centuries ago yet so appropriate for us today. I just want you to know if we had to do it all again, I wouldn't change one decision I made today."

Jessica felt like his eyes were burning a hole into her heart, and she nearly melted when he reached out and gently touched her cheek. "I'm praying you find your father, Jess."

Ben walked away, leaving Jessica to stand there staring after him. Did she hear him right? Did he call her Jess? What did that mean? Only her family and people very close to her called her that.

As she turned to find her sister and get herself settled for the night, a small smile crept up to her face. It felt good to smile. And even though Jessica still had so many unanswered questions, she managed to push them aside long enough to bring her hand up to her cheek. As she glanced back over her shoulder, she found Ben nowhere in sight.

CHAPTER 27

Jessica bolted upright with a start, her eyes wide with fear. What just happened? Looking around her, she saw families sleeping on donated blankets given by caring people who knew this place would serve as a sanctuary to so many. She looked at Ashley next to her, making sure she didn't wake her. Then she looked at Mrs. Miller on the other side of Ashley, who also was sound asleep.

Her lungs wouldn't work as she tried to calm her breathing. Then she realized what happened. It was a nightmare, one that would take her a long time to forget, where she saw her father laying, unconscious, somewhere down at the World Trade Center. She had been calling to him from behind a thick cloud but couldn't get to him. Lying back down, Jessica let the tears fall, once more.

Every time she closed her eyes and tried to fall back asleep, she would see the image. It was so real. Even with the exhaustion she was feeling, sleep wouldn't return.

As soon as the sun began to rise, Jessica decided it was time. School had already been cancelled for today, and she knew she would have at least a half hour head start if she left now.

Still in her clothes, she resolved to do just that. That way she wouldn't be met with objections. The night before, she had quietly slipped away from the group and wrote a note to Ashley with a pencil and an old math test she found in her bag. She grabbed the test and placed it quietly next to Ashley where she wouldn't miss it. Then she found her backpack with her cell phone, water, protein bar, Yankees hat, and sketchbook inside. She also included some things she might need: medical tape, gauze, and a few extra water bottles. Picking up her shoes silently, she padded her way to the door in her socks.

Once outside, Jessica couldn't believe she'd made it out without waking anyone. She silently chided herself for not heeding Pastor Dan's advice from the evening before to stay inside the church until one of her parents came. "I'm sorry, Pastor Dan. I have no choice. I know my father's in trouble and needs me."

Jessica had enough time to plan this trip through. She knew the police barricades would be up across Canal Street. She also knew school had already been cancelled, and only emergency personnel would be allowed into Lower Manhattan today. Someone had said that last night after seeing a news report on the church TV.

As she worked her way down toward Canal Street, hiding in every doorway, staying in the shadows, Jessica kept looking behind her to make sure she wasn't being followed. While she waited inside the doorway of the last building before crossing Canal Street, Jessica prayed that God would somehow allow her to get by the police officers without being seen. *Funny*, she thought, *I'm not sure God would hear a prayer that was technically illegal.* She didn't have time to think about that now. She knew what she needed to do. It was like that question her class was asked in school last year. The question revolved around a sick person who would only get better by taking a medicine that was locked up in the doctor's cabinet. The question was to cause the students to think about morals. Would you do nothing knowing the medicine was within reach, or would you break into the cabinet and steal the medicine to save the person's life?

Jessica, of course, knew what her parents would say. Trust God. He is the true Healer. But right now, in this moment, her parents weren't here, and she was. With all her heart, she believed she needed to get to her father, even if it meant going against the law.

"Mount up with wings as eagles." Whispering to herself, Jessica felt a surge of energy course through her as she felt herself relax a bit.

Amazingly, it was easy for Jessica to cross over. It was still dark enough to cast lots of shadows, and a few police officers, assuming most people were still asleep, had congregated together a little ways from where Jessica planned to cross. She didn't hesitate making her move, and bolting out of the doorway under the barricade into a shadowy doorway, she picked out while still across the street.

At this point, she was breathing so fast she needed to bend over at the waist to settle herself down. She wasn't sure if it was from running so fast or from the fear of being caught. It didn't matter. She made it this far, and now, she was met with a struggle.

Her original plan was to travel all the way down Broadway since Greene changed to Broadway south of Canal Street. The majority of rescue workers would probably travel down Broadway or West Street, and she thought she could blend in better. However, thinking about it now, she wondered if she should go a little ways down and then move one block west to Church Street where she might be able to be more discrete.

In the end, Jessica decided to stay on Broadway until she hit Leonard Street, below Sixth Avenue, and then head west to Church Street. The roads were still pretty dark and lightly traveled, so thus far, she was making good time.

The sun was rising when Jessica arrived at Warren Street, and she noticed an airplane flying overhead. Looking down for the first time, she noticed what she had been walking on. There was about two inches of dust covering every inch of street and sidewalk. She didn't know how far north it started, but this must have been what they were running away from yesterday. Her hand rose to her mouth to stifle a sob as she realized what she was standing on. This was concrete from the buildings. All around her were pieces of the Twin Towers.

It was almost more than she could bear, and a longing filled her heart as she considered making a stop at her apartment. She knew nobody would be there, and it would just delay the inevitable. The sooner she made it down to "Ground Zero," which is what the TV and radios were calling the area at the World Trade Center, the sooner she could find her father.

With one last pep talk and a deep breath, she was about to pass over her street when she heard the sound of footsteps and men talking. Quickly, she ducked around the corner and stooped down in the doorway a couple of buildings down from her own. She came this far and was almost there, so she didn't want to take any chances of being caught now.

Quietly, she pulled out her baseball cap from her backpack and tucked her hair in. *Good thing I was thinking ahead for once*, she thought. She knew her bag would be heavy, but it was worth it now in case she didn't make it back up to church before tomorrow.

Once the group of workers passed, she peeked around the corner up Church Street. *Great. More people*, she thought. Now that the day had begun, Jessica figured people would be pouring in to help. She had no choice. Pulling her jacket up to her neck, she stood tall and turned back onto Church Street joining the end of the large group that was passing by. Staying a bit behind, keeping her head up so anyone behind her would think she was with the group, she tried to disguise the way she walked to blend in but tripped over her feet and realized the safest thing would be to stay tall, walk normally, and get down there as quickly as possible.

CHAPTER 28

New York had never been like this, Buddy Powers reflected. Random people wandered the streets searching for some meaning to their life. Some still slept inside Burger King or any other safe place they could find the night before. These were the ones who found themselves stuck at ground zero, unable to get out the previous day. Coffee cups were still sitting on tables inside shops with cold coffee waiting to be drunk. Laptops still open on tables next to the coffee, ready to perform the next command entered.

Exhaustion threatened to overtake Buddy as he pulled down his mask and stood tall, giving his back a much-needed stretch. There was no time for rest. Temptation crept in to look around him, but he didn't need to. He knew what was there. He had been at this for hours, and the scene looked pretty much the same.

Teams of strangers torn away unannounced from their separate roads of life now joined together with one mission: to assemble down at "Ground Zero" and rescue survivors. Buddy's team rotated with the other four, taking turns descending down into the pit of a once-massive structure, now only a massive heap of rubble.

The teams consisted of steel workers, a rescue dog, and a physician. Each team had a Jaws of Life tool to help them. Buddy recalled the phone call his boss received just hours earlier. He only heard one side of it, but it was very clear their mission was to remove the heaps of steel so other rescue workers could help the people who were trapped underneath.

Ironically, the first victim Buddy found was a first responder. He was a firefighter whose bravery and courage will be remembered by his family as they bury him.

Coughing, Buddy pulled his mask over his face and continued with his work. He felt a hand on his shoulder and turned to find the next team ready to take over. Buddy's eyes smiled at the man as he patted his back, turning to ascend the stairwell that led out of the pit. Stepping over human remains, Buddy mourned for each soul that would never see another sunrise.

Reaching the top, Buddy made his way to the row of tables adorned with food. He would be eternally grateful to all the restaurants and individual people who gave food to feed him. However, he also struggled with feelings of worthiness. Who was he that he should eat of this food. He was nobody in the world's eye. Yet here he was, smack in the center of it all.

He scooped himself some food from Olive Garden and found a place to sit. The eerie silence was one of the only motivators that kept Buddy going for hours on end. Nobody talked, but there was an underlying sense of American pride and determination. The silence was all right with him though. It gave him more opportunity to pray. Bowing his head, Buddy prayed for his food just like he had been doing for years. This time, however, he extended his prayer. *Just one, Lord. Help me to find just one person alive to help.*

CHAPTER 29

M r. Bianchi moaned and tried to put his hand to his head, but he couldn't move his arm. This caused him to open his eyes to see what the matter was, but when he opened them, he quickly closed them again. His head hurt—badly. Why? He couldn't remember what happened. He tried to open his eyes again but saw nothing. There was blackness. *Where am I?* He couldn't for the life of him figure out where he was.

He tried to lift his arm again. Something was on it. As he became more conscious, he began to feel it— pain, in his right arm. In fact, the pain radiated from his hand all the way up to his shoulder. He tried moving his other arm but that wouldn't move either. What was going on? He tried to move his left arm again. Then he felt something on his stomach. He realized his left arm was under his body. He tried to pull it out but felt an intense pain in his left shoulder that caused him to cry out.

As he opened his eyes again, there was the same blackness. Feeling his heart beating rapidly, Anthony Bianchi felt himself doing something he hadn't done in over twenty years—he was panicking. All of a sudden everything seemed to be closing in on him. He couldn't breathe. When he tried to call out, his mouth was so dry, and when he licked his lips, he felt grit.

Slowly, as if in slow motion, pictures started flashing through his mind, and Mr. Bianchi began to remember the terror that had taken place. He had no idea what day it was or how long he had been knocked out. But the facts began taking shape, and he remembered bringing a woman to safety. What was her name? Oh well, it didn't matter. He knew where he was, somewhere between his office building and World Trade Center Tower 2. His stomach churned as he wondered if anything was left of it. And then another thought came to his mind—his family. Were they safe? Where were they? Was anyone looking for him? Did they think he was dead? He began to feel the terror of that last thought, but just as quickly, he remembered Jeremiah 29 and began reciting it in his mind. *Thoughts of peace... plans to give you a future and a hope...*

A future and a hope. These words caused Mr. Bianchi to feel a sense of inner peace and strength that was gone a minute ago. He tried to roll over so he could free his arm, but there was something above him that blocked him from moving at all. Well, if he couldn't move, there was only one thing left to do. He tried to spit out some of the pieces of whatever was in his mouth and lick his lips as he grimaced from the taste and feel of it between his lips and attempted to call out.

"HELP!" It seemed so loud in his head, but his ears heard nothing. He licked his lips again. Oh, if only he could have some water. *No, I can't think about that right now. If I can call for help, then I will be able to get some water.* He tried again. "HELP!" This time, he heard a voice that sounded like a faint whisper. A voice that he didn't recognize.

God, your plans for me include a future and a hope. Please, help me now. Hear my prayer, O Lord, and let my cry come to you.

The last part surprised him. Psalm 102 was a chapter he had used earlier in his life during some dark times, but he hadn't needed it lately. He had just about forgotten about it until it came to the front of his memory. He continued, *Do not hide your face from me in the day of my trouble; Incline your ear to me; In the day that I call, answer me speedily.* After wetting his lips, Mr. Bianchi tried again. "HELP!" This time, he heard it! It still didn't sound like his voice, but he heard it all the same! "HELP!" He called again several more times, each time a little louder and with more confidence than before.

Finally, when he was too out of breath and about to give up, he heard something. It sounded like it came from very nearby. He tried to quiet his heartbeat so he could hear. Yes! It was a voice! Mr. Bianchi gathered all the strength that was left in him and one last time called for help.

This time he got a response. "We hear you! Don't worry. We are going to try to remove the debris on top of you so we can help you. What's your name?"

Mr. Bianchi had barely enough strength to speak, but somehow, he managed. "Anthony Bianchi. I work in the Deutsche Bank Building. Or I did. Before…"

"Okay, Mr. Bianchi, welcome back! Help is on its way!"

Mr. Bianchi laid his head down and smiled. He knew in just a short while, once again, God would complete another miracle.

CHAPTER 30

As Jessica approached Barclay Street without being stopped (she had no idea how that happened, besides divine intervention), her feet suddenly felt heavier than concrete bricks. She stopped in her tracks as she could only stare at the scene unfolding in front of her. "Oh…my…gosh" was all she could gasp. No thought had been given to what it would look like down here. Concentrating on only the thought about finding her father, she now realized that she was right in front of the effects of the terror, causing her to question herself.

"What am I doing here? I don't belong here at all." The once familiar place of enjoyment for her and her family was no more. In its place was chaos and masses of steel bent to create a structure so intimidating that it seemed like some sort of monster. Determined beings moved on and around the structure, and some were even inside it. Nobody spoke, but they all seemed to work together in unison with the same mission. After giving herself a pep talk, Jessica inhaled deeply and crossed the street.

She wanted to begin at her father's office building just in case he was trapped somewhere over there. As she crossed Vesey Street, her eyes found the steeple of St. Paul's Chapel and made their way down to the doorway. *Unbelievable*, she thought. *All this destruction surrounding us, and this little chapel stands strong, untouched.* Jessica reflected on this for a minute, struck by the greatness of God. Even though she had lived in New York all her life, she had never been inside this building. She made a mental note to change that. Her eyes then traveled down to the cemetery out front, and she was saddened to see here too was that thick layer of concrete dust.

Jessica began feeling a little strange. The chapel became blurry to her, and she felt like she was on a ride at Coney Island. Just when she thought her legs would no longer hold her upright, she felt arms around her. She found herself looking up into the face of a man probably her father's age, covered in dust wearing a hardhat.

"Whoa there, young lady, take it easy. What's a girl like you doing down here? This is no place for someone like you. Where's your…"

Jessica never heard the rest of the man's question. The next thing she knew, everything was foggy. *No, please don't let me pass out. I've come too far to be sent back now. It's too late, Jessica. You've already been discovered. They won't let you stay here anyway.* These thoughts battled for the forefront of her mind, and then there was nothing at all.

≈

When Jessica woke, possibly minutes, or hours, later, she was laying on something hard. She sat up and looked around. A church. St. Paul's Chapel, she guessed. There were lots of pews in rows around her just like the one she was lying on. She saw a small altar on the other side of the room. Up above her was another level with seats and what looked like an organ.

But what really struck her was the small group of people gathered near the pulpit. Just above them was the most beautiful chandelier she had ever laid eyes on. It wasn't the beauty of the chapel that she was interested in at the moment. Rather it was what the group was talking about. Most of them were in normal everyday clothes, and they didn't look at all dirty. Before she could attempt to sneak out, the man who came to her rescue earlier spotted her. He excused himself from the group heading her way, and she wasn't sure if she should run or pretend not to see him.

He made sure to walk extra slowly, mulling the details of his thoughts around in his brain until he could figure out the best way to approach the young girl sitting just a few yards away. What are the odds that she crossed his path just at the same time he was making his way over to the chapel. If he hadn't received the call from one of the volunteers, he would have still been over helping his fellow rescue workers.

"Feeling better?" He smiled and sat down on the pew next to her. He seemed to be in his mid-sixties with more grey in his hair than black. His was a friendly fatherly voice, the kind that made her want to curl up and cry.

"A little, I guess. Thank you." Jessica felt so uncomfortable and out of place that she missed her parents all the more.

"Well, that's good. Where are you from?"

"Warren Street." Jessica barely got the words out. She wanted to tell him more, tell him about her father and her reason for being down here, but nothing else came out.

"Ah yes, just up the street a bit. How did you come to find yourself down here when the mayor evacuated everyone yesterday? By the way, my name's Buddy Powers." Buddy offered his hand for Jessica to shake.

Remembering her manners, she replied, "Jessica Bianchi. Nice to meet you, Mr. Powers." She noticed a change in Buddy's expression, but he let out a laugh that sounded fake even to him.

"Mr. Powers is my father. Please think of me as your rescue buddy and just call me Buddy. Now, Ms. Bianchi, care to tell me your story?"

Jessica didn't know how, but she managed to find the strength to get through the entire story from start to finish in record's time. No detail was left out including the strain in her relationship with her father and her desire to make it right. Buddy listened intently the entire time. As she finished, she was nervous to look at him, afraid she might see anger in his eyes at her disobedience. But she saw only love and something else she couldn't quite put her finger on.

"Well, let's figure out how to get you back where it's safe. As I told you before, this is no place for a young lady to be right now. Why don't you tell me your father's name and what he looks like, and I'll see what I can do. We are a little busy right now trying to get this place set up as a refuge for rescue workers only, but I believe God put me here at the same time you needed me. So I want to help you."

Jessica swallowed back the emotion that threatened to rise in her and reached down for her backpack to retrieve her sketchbook. A few months ago, she had done a sketch of her father at a summer picnic, and it was still in her book. But she couldn't find her bag. Buddy knew the moment of truth had come.

"Oh yeah, I almost forgot." He slowly rose and went to the foyer to retrieve her bag. He brought it over to her but began his explanation as he extended it to Jessica. "After you fainted, I thought it best to try to contact a family member. I looked through your bag for some sort of information or ID card." He pulled out her sketchbook. "I also found this." He handed it to her, almost embarrassed to have looked through something so personal to this young girl.

"Thank you" was all she said as she avoided looking at him.

"Is there a picture of your father in there?" Buddy held his breath as the next words spoken would confirm what he already knew to be true.

"Yes, I sketched one of him just a couple months ago." As she flipped open the cover, she watched her trembling fingers. She looked up and noticed Buddy watching her too. "Uh, it's just right here, let me see, it was one I did recently." As she began to flip, her eyes rested on the sketches she had done after her lunch at Windows on the World. The picture of David, her server, was first. Her breath caught in her throat as she looked at his face. She hadn't even thought of David. She was sure he must be dead.

"A friend of yours?" Buddy's voice broke into her thoughts, not in a harsh way, but in a sympathetic tone, almost like he knew what she was thinking.

"Um, not really." Jessica quickly flipped the pages to the back. "He was a server at Windows on the World restaurant. My parents took me there in April for my birthday, and I had only seen him that once…" Her voice trailed off, and she attempted to recompose herself before finding her father's picture. "There." She pointed to it. "Anthony Bianchi." Buddy noticed the resemblance immediately even though it was just a sketch. "Of course, it's just a rough sketch," Jessica stammered.

Buddy looked up and thought what his face must have looked like to her. "And a fine one at that. I'd recognize him anywhere. The resemblance is uncanny."

Jessica wrinkled her eyebrows in confusion. "What do you mean? Do you know him?"

Buddy knew he couldn't put it off any longer. "Only briefly. In fact"—Buddy cleared his throat and willed his eyes to meet Jessica's—"I met him just a little while ago."

"Oh?" Jessica seemed confused at his behavior. "Did he take you to lunch? Are you one of his clients?"

"Not exactly." *God, you gave me this assignment. Give me the words.* "I literally just met him a little while ago. Me and some other guys found him under a piece of metal just minutes before I headed over here."

Buddy could see Jessica's expression turn from confusion to shock and then to complete joy. "You mean he's alive? You found him? Where is he?" The questions couldn't come out fast enough. "You have to take me to him. I have to see him!" Jessica moved to stand up, but she stood too quickly and the room began to spin. Just as quickly as she stood, she sat down again.

"Please, please take me to him. I can't leave here without knowing he's okay." The tears came then, first in small broken sobs, and then in floods of emotion. Buddy was never comfortable in situations like this, and he wasn't sure what to do. He scratched the back of his neck and hesitantly extended his arm to comfort Jessica. Her actions assured him it was the right move, for as soon as she felt it, she buried her face into his shirt. He knew he should tell her the rest, but not yet. Mr. Bianchi had passed out again shortly after Buddy talked to him. The men feared him dead. It was just a waiting game now to see if and when Mr. Bianchi woke. There would be time enough to fill Jessica in on the details. Right now, she needed to rejoice in the knowledge that her father was found, and alive—God willing.

CHAPTER 31

Mr. Bianchi woke once more to darkness. This time, he heard the voices talking, but he couldn't feel anything below his neck. He began to call out for someone to hear him, but the voices seemed so far away. Just then, a bright light shone above him. He wondered if he was in heaven. The light quickly disappeared, and the voices seemed louder and closer.

"Mr. Bianchi, you awake?" It was a man's voice but unfamiliar to him.

"Yes, but I can't feel my body. Please help me." Mr. Bianchi remembered the details of where he was, but last he remembered, men were beginning to rescue him. "What happened?" He wanted answers.

The same gentleman replied, "You passed out again, man. We need you to stay awake for us. We've got someone coming who can hopefully cut this metal off you. But we don't want to lose you again. Keep talkin' for us."

Mr. Bianchi was having a hard time breathing with his arm under him, but he craned his head as much as he could and called out, "Okay, I'll try, but I'm running out of strength fast. How long have I been out?"

"Since the first time we talked to you? About five minutes. Long enough for us to think we might have to call the missus, if there is one. Tell me about your family."

Smart man, Mr. Bianchi thought. He knew this was a tactic to keep him awake. He knew the seriousness of passing out after a fall and not waking up again. He had been taught that much during his athletic days. Knowing that God was bigger than some metal, he said a quick silent prayer and began telling the men about his beloved family, whom he hoped to see very soon.

～

Jessica brought her hand to her head in response to a nagging ache she felt. She was fighting against the tears once more, but this time, it was in reaction to the news Buddy had just given her. *What if he doesn't wake up again?* No. She wouldn't allow those thoughts to enter her mind. "Can you bring me there?" She already knew the answer to her question, but she felt the need to ask it just the same.

"Now you know I can't very well do that." Buddy regretted having to tell her this. He wished there was something he could do.

"Then can I stay here while you go back, and when he is rescued, you can bring him here." This was more of a statement than a question. Jessica was hopeful, and she knew it would work if Buddy just agreed to it.

Buddy only shook his head and scratched his chin. Jessica noticed he was looking down, avoiding any eye contact with her. "I can't do that either. This place is strictly for rescue workers."

Jessica was about to argue, but Buddy had another idea. "Tell you what, I'll see what I can do, and in the meantime, why don't we get you upstairs out of the way so you can rest." He didn't have to ask twice. With a nod, Jessica allowed herself to be helped up off the bench and made her way upstairs.

It wasn't long before one of the women she recognized from the small group brought her a tray of food and drink. "Well, young lady, someone is smiling down on you today. One of the rules here is no children are permitted while we are helping the survivors and rescuers. However, after talking with Buddy, you are in no condition to take a step outside this chapel until you feel better. Here, why don't you take something to eat? By the way, my name is Betty. Buddy had to go back out but asked me to keep a watch over you. How are you feeling?"

Jessica's mind felt hazy, and she told Betty so. "But you don't understand, I need to go—"

Betty cut her off. "You are not going anywhere, my dear. And Buddy filled me in on the whole story. You will see your father soon enough. Right now, you need to rest. Otherwise, you'll find yourself in a worse situation than him." Before Jessica could argue, Betty turned to head back downstairs to help the constant stream of workers.

Jessica sat up slowly to drink and thought about her mother. She would want to know that her husband was safe. Reaching into her bag, her hand found her cell phone. A thank-you to God escaped her lips as she saw that it was almost fully charged. Panic filled her, however, as she unlocked it. No service. Of course. The cell phone service was provided by the antennae on top of the Twin Towers. She felt truly alone.

CHAPTER 32

Storm clouds barreled across the clear blue sky at lightning speed. The coolness that resulted sent a shiver up Jessica's spine. Her eyes fixated on something far in the distance. It started out as a tiny brown speck. *It's growing bigger*, Jessica thought to herself. As the speck grew, she realized it was growing bigger because it seemed to be coming toward her. She followed it as it ascended higher and higher above the clouds. Just when it was almost directly above her did she realize what it was. The feathers blew against the wind, and Jessica watched as the eagle turned its body and soared higher and higher, effortlessly, resting on the wind.

Peace filled her as the eagle continued rising. Something caused her to look down below the storm clouds. While panic threatened to push the peaceful feeling out, Jessica clung to it desperately though why, she didn't know. Just as she relaxed and felt her body almost floating through the air, *crash!*

Jessica must have fallen asleep because she awoke with a start to what seemed like a loud crash. Her body was drenched in sweat, and her breathing was faster than normal. Something had awoken her, but it was at the same time that she heard the plane crashing into the North Tower in her dream. Looking around her, she momentarily didn't remember where she was. Then it all came back to her. She was just yards away from her father. Oh, yes, she was upstairs inside St. Paul's Chapel. Exhausted and grabbing the railing, she looked over and saw what must have woken her. Several rescue workers were lying across the pews, sleeping, and one fireman's hat fell off the pew, echoing as it hit the floor. As Jessica examined the workers, dread crept up. They all looked the same, covered in gray dust, and even their faces and hands were unrecognizable. They had come here for a few moment's rest before going back out to help.

Sadness washed over her. As she took in every inch of the scene below, she thought about how much things had changed in just one day. How many people had lost a parent or relative? Jessica once again felt guilt not only for the way she treated her father, but also for being so selfish and not thinking about others around her and how their lives had been affected. *God, forgive me. Help me to remember others before myself.*

After she prayed, she remembered something. Her parents had often talked about love, and one of the most important things about loving others is putting oneself last. She silently committed herself to putting her heart into helping as much as possible until she saw her father again.

Feeling better, she attempted to try her phone again. Of course there was no change. All she wanted at that moment was to be safe in her mother's arms. She recalled Proverbs 3:5, another of her mother's favorite verses. Jessica knew it well. She whispered it aloud as she tried to compose herself. "Trust in the Lord with all your heart, and lean not on your own understanding. In all your ways acknowledge Him, and He will direct your paths."

Looking to the door as it opened, Jessica searched the group hoping to see a familiar face. But all she saw was more of the same. Turning from the railing, Jessica attempted to head downstairs and see if she could help do something, even if it was just pass out cups of water for the workers coming in.

As she reached the bottom, she listened to various conversations around her while she looked for Betty. Two workers were talking about how the FBI set up a Web site for tips for people looking for a loved one and a phone number for family and friends of victims to call, leaving their contact information. Jessica felt relief at not having to remember that number, expecting to see her father soon.

She felt better with each step she took, even though she was exhausted. She looked around for Betty, but not finding her, she decided to go back upstairs to stay out of the way. Since she did not see Buddy either, she could only hope he was still rescuing her father.

CHAPTER 33

The next couple hours passed so slowly that Jessica wondered if time stopped. Her thoughts traveled to David, wondering if he was still alive, to Mrs. West and her husband. Every so often she would look over the railing to the first floor and her eye would scan the pews, looking for one particular face. Jessica felt her stomach rumble and decided to once more head downstairs to see if she could find Betty. Walking by the doorway that led to the cemetery, she glanced toward the door hoping to see it open up revealing her father on the other side. But, as she half expected, it opened only to a group of men she didn't recognize. They were all covered with dust, which did not surprise her, although she still didn't think she could stomach much of the sight. The lead man in front stamped his feet outside before entering. Looking for water and something to eat, she continued on when something behind him caught the corner of her eye. She slowly backed up and saw a man lying on a home-made stretcher between two tall men. He was covered with dust and had bandages on both his shoulders and along his right arm. His eyes were closed, but something about his features caused Jessica's heart to stop.

Everything else faded into the background. Slowly and cautiously, she approached the men carrying the stretcher through the door, wanting to make sure she was seeing what she was hoping for. She looked up at the tallest man, and as he smiled, her eyes held a deep gratitude to him as she recognized the eyes of Buddy. The tears came uncontrollably even before she got out the one word she wanted to say.

"Dad?"

The man opened his eyes just enough to see, and his reply, though it was weak, was all she needed to know they would be okay.

"Hey, Peanut."

EPILOGUE

Jessica gently pushed her plate away. She was stuffed. Nestling back against the soft cushioned chair, she looked around the elegant room. Tonight was a dinner for the men and women who bravely offered their lives to help in the hours and days after the attacks. Looking at the faces around the table talking and laughing, Jessica closed her eyes in an attempt to remember the emotion in each face so she could sketch it later in her room.

"Jess, are you all right, dear?" She smiled before opening her eyes as the now familiar voice of her grandmother whispered into her ear.

Nodding her head in reply, Jessica opened her eyes to the warm, wrinkled eyes of her Mémé smiling back at her.

It was hard to believe only a little over one month had passed since the tragic events of September 11. In one short month, Jessica felt like she was an entire year or two older. She allowed herself to remember back to those first few days after the event.

Once she found her father, she made an attempt to patch up the relationship and strengthen it even more than it had ever been. Of course it didn't hurt that he was in the hospital for a time after. She knew their relationship may have more ups and downs, but she would never take her father for granted again. Well, she would try not to.

Once her father was settled in his hospital bed, Buddy helped Jessica get back to church and share the news with her sister and her church family. She didn't know how she would have gotten along without Buddy. Sitting in between her father and herself, Buddy looked sharp in his rented suit.

For four days after the attacks, Mr. Bianchi remained in the hospital. The plan was to get the apartment ready for his return home with Mrs. Bianchi (who managed to find an alternate route home the evening after the attacks) and her girls remaining at the church until his discharge. Of course, Jessica learned man's plans aren't always God's plans. Upon arriving at the apartment later that same day, they were informed it was deemed unlivable. Concrete dust had overtaken the building, as with many other apartment buildings in lower Manhattan. Heading once more to church, the family remained there for another four days until the cleanup had been completed.

Jessica remembered how she didn't really mind, however, staying at the church since Ben and his mother also had to stay out of their apartment for cleaning. Mrs. Bianchi and Mrs. Miller seemed to get along well, and Mr. Miller was very grateful to the Bianchi's for providing shelter for his family while he was away.

On the other side of Mr. Bianchi sat Jessica's mother. How pretty she looked with her hair pulled up like that. Jessica noticed how her mother laid her hand on her husband's arm. One touch said a thousand words. Jessica knew the trials her mother faced, forced to stay away from her family for what seemed like the longest day of her life. She knew how hard it was for her mother to be an entire state away, and while she could only guess how her faith was tested, she also knew how divine intervention played a role in her grandparents' presence during that time.

This last thought turned Jessica's mind to her grandparents, seated also at the table. Mrs. Bianchi's parents remained in New Jersey with their daughter until she could get back to the city. That was why they were still here, extending their vacation indefinitely to make sure their daughter and her family were okay.

Of course, upon their arrival home the following day, they would be very busy with packing and getting things prepared for the move. Jessica smiled again as she replayed the conversation Mémé and Papa had with the family about how the events of that day led them to reprioritize their lives. They realized how much they missed out on the girls' lives, and this ultimately led to the decision to sell the ranch and move to the city. Mrs. Bianchi broke into tears, and the girls squeezed their grandparents as to never let them go.

September 2001 proved to be a month of terrible heartache and sadness, death and destruction. However, amidst all that awfulness, one beautiful thing was born. The bonds of love that ran so deep between family members were strengthened so tight they could never be cut again.

AFTERWORD

Almost 3000 people died in the World Trade Center disaster; 343 were firefighters and paramedics, 23 were New York City Police, and 37 were Port Authority Police. Jessica's story is fictional, as are all the characters. However, it is one that could have very likely happened to a young girl living in New York City during that time. Even though Jessica found her father fairly quickly, this was not the case in many instances. The FBI established a phone number for loved ones to call, leaving information just in case someone was found days or weeks later.

The schools and church are fictional as well. Tribeca's Tasties is not a real sweet shop. However, it is in the location of Tribeca Treats, a charming dessert shop that sells delicious treats.

New York City was affected in so many ways that day, and it would take a long time for some sort of normalcy to return. The New York Stock Exchange was closed until September 17. The Holland Tunnel was closed for one month after 9/11 except for emergency vehicles. Subways closed down, and all trains didn't resume their normal schedule until October 28. No vehicles were permitted south of Canal Street until October 13. Not only was Lower Manhattan evacuated, but the White House, the Capital building, Sears Tower in Chicago, 1 DS Center in Minneapolis, and the Mall of America in Minnesota all were evacuated that day.

Many lives were interrupted as people gathered from all parts of the country to help search and rescue victims. Included in this list were steel workers, nurses, police officers, firefighters, and Red Cross workers, just to name a few. Special thanks to one person in particular, Jennifer Fimiani, whose personal experiences helped give me a better understanding of the nightmare of those first days after the attacks.

Our country came together that day as one united nation. The bonds that were created will surely remain strong in the years to come.